Also by Gillian Cross

The Furry Maccaloo
The Monster from Underground
The Tree House
What Will Emily Do?

for older readers

Born of the Sun
Gobbo the Great
A Map of Nowhere
The Mintyglo Kid
Save Our School
Swimathon!

The Crazy Shoe Shuffle

Gillian Cross

Illustrated by Nick Sharratt

mammoth

First published in Great Britain 1995
by Methuen Children's Books Ltd
Published 1996 by Mammoth
an imprint of Egmont Children's Books Ltd
Michelin House, 81 Fulham Road, London SW3 6RB

Reprinted 1996 (twice), 1997, 1998 (twice)

Text copyright © 1995 Gillian Cross
Illustrations copyright © 1995 Nick Sharratt

The right of Gillian Cross and Nick Sharratt to be identified
as author and illustrator of this work has been asserted by them
in accordance with the Copyright, Designs and Patents Act 1988

ISBN 0 7497 2200 2

A CIP catalogue record for this title
is available from the British Library

Printed and bound in Great Britain
by Cox & Wyman Ltd, Reading, Berkshire

Contents

1 *The Shoe Mountain*

It was an awful day, even before the trouble with the shoes. The weather was damp and grey and freezing cold, and everything went wrong.

First of all, Lee lost his football.

He often brought it on Mondays, because Mr Willoughby was on playground duty, and he let them play football at break, as long as Mr Merton didn't see. They were wonderful games and Lee spent the whole week looking forward to them.

But that morning he made a fatal mistake. Instead of carrying the ball in his bag, he dribbled it along the pavement, all the way to school. And when he reached the gate Mr Merton was there.

Lee bent down to snatch up the ball and jam it into his bag, but he was too late. Mr Merton's long, pale fingers closed round it.

'*I'll* take care of this,' he said.

'Oh, sir!' It was Lee's only football.

Mr Merton smiled his thin, tight smile. 'You know the rules. No football in the playground.'

'But I wasn't *in* the playground!'

Mr Merton didn't bother to answer. He just pointed at the spot where the ball had been lying. Two inches inside the gate. Then he tucked it under his arm and walked away.

Fred Askew hadn't missed that. He never missed anything. The moment Mr Merton was gone, he came bounding across to Lee. 'That was stupid. You won't get it back, you know. Not till the end of term.'

'Shut up!' Lee growled. It was only January. The end of term was a long way away.

But Fred didn't shut up. He enjoyed being cleverer than everyone else, and he always went on and on about things. 'Bet old Merton's got *millions* of footballs at home. Bet he kicks them all round his garden every night.'

'Don't be daft,' Peanuts said, from the ground near their feet. She was upside-down, doing a handstand against the railings, but she always had to disagree with Fred. 'Mr Merton can't play football. He's got creaky knees. Look at him.'

They all looked. Mr Merton was just climbing the steps, and Lee could see how carefully he went. Peanuts was right. His knees looked very stiff. Somehow that made it even worse. The football wasn't any use to *him*. Why did he have to take it?

Peanuts flipped the right way up and tweaked Lee's tie out of his jumper. 'Why don't you tell Miss Cherry? Burst into tears and make her feel sorry for you. I bet she can get it back.'

'Ha ha,' Lee said, scowling.

But it was too late. Peanuts had decided on her joke for the day. All the morning, she kept pulling miserable faces across the classroom at him.

'*Go on!*' she mouthed. '*Boo hoo, boo hoo, boo hoo!*'

Miss Cherry didn't notice her. Peanuts was very good at not being noticed. But Lee wasn't so lucky.

'Shove off, Peanuts!' he hissed, when he finally lost his temper. He pulled a horrible, ugly face – and then turned round and saw Miss Cherry looking reproachfully at him.

'*Lee*! That's not very nice.'

She wasn't angry, because she never got angry, but that just made Lee feel worse. He went red. 'I was only – '

Miss Cherry shook her head at him and her shiny blonde curls bounced round her face. 'You know I don't like nastiness in my class. I didn't think you were like that. I thought you were a helpful, dependable boy.'

That made Lee feel about two centimetres tall. So when Miss Cherry asked for someone to stay behind after school and clean out the hamster cage, he stuck his hand up straight away, to show that he really was helpful and dependable. Miss Cherry beamed at him and by the time he remembered he'd promised to be home early, it was too late to back out.

He couldn't let Miss Cherry down.

Dinner-time was the next disaster. They were the last class to get into dinner and by the time Lee reached the front of the queue there was nothing left except disgusting stew. He took his share, but the moment he tasted it he knew he'd choke if he ate it. He spread it round the plate and tried to hide it under his knife and fork.

And Mrs Puddock, the Head, chose that moment to come swooping through the Hall, on the way to her office. The moment she saw his plate, she pounced.

'Lee Godwin, don't you DARE leave all that good food.'

'I can't help it,' Lee muttered. 'It's horrible.'

Mrs Puddock put her hands on her hips, towering over Lee like an all-in wrestler. 'This isn't a hotel, you know. In *my* school, you eat what you're given. And I'm going to stand here and make sure you do.'

She did. She stood over him, with her huge red face glaring down, while he

struggled to swallow the tough, gristly meat. He was nearly sick three times, but he had to sit there all the way through dinner playtime, until he'd finished every last mouthful.

And that made him late for Games.

Normally, Games was the best bit of Mondays, but not today. When he ran out onto the field – five minutes late – Mr Merton looked sourly at him.

'I thought you liked football, Lee. But you can't even be bothered to get here in time. You'd better go in goal.'

It was a totally foul day. *Everything* had gone wrong. Even the hamster bit him. By the time he had finished cleaning out the cage and slammed the door shut, he just wanted to get out of school and go home.

And that was when he walked down to the cloakroom, with Miss Cherry close behind him. And saw the shoe mountain.

'Oh *Lee*!' Miss Cherry shook her head, and her shoulders drooped pathetically. 'Just look at that!'

Lee looked.

The cloakroom was full of jumbled shoes. Someone had taken all the indoor shoes out of people's shoe-bags and dumped them in a heap on the floor. There must have been well over a hundred pairs – pumps and trainers, slippers and lace-ups, shiny new sandals and battered old baseball boots all piled up higgledy-piggledy.

'Oh *dear*,' Miss Cherry said.

Her big blue eyes looked helplessly at Lee, and he sighed. He didn't *want* to clear up all those shoes. But everyone else had gone home. And he couldn't leave Miss Cherry to do it on her own.

Could he?

She looked at the shoes and shook her head again, and the long, fair curls bobbed round her face. 'We can't just leave them there. There'll be chaos in the morning. And you know what Mrs Puddock's like.'

She looked sideways at Lee, with a little, secret smile. *We know about Mrs Puddock, don't we?* the smile said. And Lee found himself smiling back.

Then Miss Cherry looked down at her watch and sighed. 'I suppose I'll just have to pick them all up. And miss playing badminton.' She sighed again. 'That will make three weeks running.'

Lee wriggled awkwardly. He was late already. But he couldn't leave her clearing up on her own.

'Suppose I help – ?' he began, gruffly.

Miss Cherry beamed at him. 'Oh, thank you! What a kind boy you are!' Before Lee could blink, she was pulling on her coat. 'I hope it doesn't take you too long.'

He hadn't meant to do it all by himself, but there was no time to explain that. Before he could say another word, Miss Cherry was out in the car park, unlocking her car. And he was left looking down at the shoes.

He took a long, deep breath and shook his head. He could guess who'd chucked them all on the floor. Peanuts. Or Fred. It was just the sort of thing those two thought was funny.

Well, they were going to be sorry.

He rummaged through the pile until he found their shoes. He knew they'd be there. Both of them were too clever to give themselves away by missing out their own. Fred's shiny black lace-ups were halfway down, and Peanuts' flashy trainers – with the green felt-pen blot on the right toe – were at the very bottom.

Lee pushed both pairs into his own

shoe-bag. When he'd finished tidying the cloakroom, he'd think of a really good place to dump them. The dustbins maybe, or the tadpole pond. Or perhaps the mud slide on the far side of the field. Somewhere really messy . . .

He thought about it while he was clearing up the other shoes. By the time he'd pushed the last pair into the right bag he'd almost decided on the scummy, smelly pond. That would be a laugh. Would the shoes float for a bit? Or would they sink straight away, into the mud?

He never had a chance to find out. He was just sitting down to change into his own outdoor shoes when a huge bellow rocked the cloakroom, shaking him where he sat.

'Lee Godwin, you HORRIBLE little boy – what are you doing NOW?'

Mrs Puddock was standing in the corridor, glaring down between the rows of pegs. Her great fat arms were full of books and her great red face was twisted into a scowl.

'Well?' she barked.

Lee swallowed. 'I was just – '

She didn't listen, of course. 'No excuses! I want you out of the school NOW!'

It was no good trying to explain. Explaining to Mrs Puddock was like trying to argue with a ten-ton truck. Lee grabbed his coat, grabbed his shoe-bag – no time to change his shoes now – and squeezed out of the cloakroom.

Mrs Puddock stood and watched him walking down the corridor. 'Get a move on!' she yelled. 'Or do I have to chase you?'

Lee started to jog towards the door. As he went, he glanced nervously over his shoulder, in case she was serious.

That was a bad mistake because he went through the door without looking. And he didn't see who was standing just outside. Before he could stop himself, he had fallen over Mr Merton's feet.

He crashed to the ground as the door slammed shut behind him.

'Well, well,' said Mr Merton. There was a sarcastic smile on his narrow, waxy face. 'In a hurry, were you?'

Lee swallowed and sat up. 'I – '

'Maybe you'd better go in and come out again. Slowly.'

Lee dragged himself to his feet. 'But Mrs Puddock – '

Mr Merton's eyebrows went up. 'What has Mrs Puddock got to do with it? Did she *push* you through the door?'

'No, but – ' Lee wriggled. Mr Merton was staring at him like a snake, and he just couldn't get the words out.

Mr Merton raised his hand and pointed. 'Go in. And come out again.'

Lee sighed and pushed the door open, as quietly as he could. There was no sign of Mrs Puddock. Slipping into the school, he turned to close the door – and the shoe-bag in his hand swung against it, with a loud thud.

Immediately, Mrs Puddock was there. She came shooting out of her office and when she saw Lee, her face went purple.

'I told you to get *OUT*!'

Lee stepped back against the closed door. 'But Mr Merton – '

'OUT!'

Lee hesitated for a second, and Mrs

Puddock started down the corridor towards him. It was like being charged by a mad bull wearing a flowery tent. Automatically – desperately – he wrenched the door open. He flung himself through it, backwards.

And fell over Mr Merton's feet again.

2 *Stolen!*

For a moment, Lee couldn't bear it. He just closed his eyes and lay there, thinking, *It hasn't happened. It's not true.* Then he looked up and saw the icy grey eyes staring down at him.

'Trouble with your legs?' Mr Merton said, acidly. 'Or is it trouble with your brain? You've never been very strong in the brain department, have you?'

'I –'

'Oh no!' Mr Merton held up his long, narrow hand. 'Don't try to talk *and* move. Your brain will never manage both at once. Just get up.'

Lee obeyed. Like a robot.

'*Very* good,' Mr Merton said sarcastically. 'Now go in and come out properly.'

'But –'

'*In.*'

Sighing, Lee pushed the door open. He knew just what he was going to see, and he did. Mrs Puddock was standing four-square in the corridor, waiting for him. As the door opened, so did her mouth. She yelled so loudly that Lee jumped and dropped his shoe-bag.

'Lee Godwin, you are a naughty, disobedient boy. Get out of this school THIS INSTANT – otherwise, I'll be round to see your parents.'

Lee couldn't believe it. He turned back to Mr Merton. Surely he'd understand now?

Mr Merton's eyes flickered. He understood all right, but he didn't smile. 'You are a silly boy, aren't you?' he murmured. 'Fancy wasting our time like that. Perhaps we'd better waste a bit of your time in return.'

Lee closed his eyes and waited for the next disaster.

'I think you ought to write – a poem,' Mr Merton said, thoughtfully. 'By tomorrow morning. A poem with at least twelve lines. And rhymes.'

Lee swallowed. 'Twelve lines about

what?'

'Let me see.' Mr Merton looked round for inspiration and saw Lee's shoe-bag on the ground. With a small, thin smile, he picked it up and turned it over in his hands. 'A poem about feet, I think.'

Twelve lines, with rhymes, about *feet*? Lee stared. 'But I can't – '

'Oh yes you can,' Mrs Puddock snapped. 'And you can put a name on that thing, too.' She nodded at the shoe-bag in Mr Merton's hands. 'You know everything you bring to school has to be named.'

'Naming things saves *such* a lot of trouble,' murmured Mr Merton. He handed the shoe-bag back to Lee. 'You can show me the name in the morning. When you give your poem in.'

Lee scowled. He wanted to say that his shoe-bag was named already, inside. But Mrs Puddock glared and Mr Merton blinked his cold eyes – and he couldn't speak. He just wanted to be at home, and he turned and ran.

He tore across the playground and out of the gate, with the bag banging against his legs. By the time he reached the shops, he was out of breath, but he didn't stop. He swung straight round the corner into the Arcade —

And fell over somebody else.

'Incher got no eyes?' yelled a shrill, cracked voice as he crashed to the ground.

It was the dirtiest old woman he had ever seen. Her long, grey hair was tangled over her shoulders, her wrinkles were grimy black lines and her clothes were bundled one on top of the other, with gaping holes that showed the layers underneath. In spite of the cold, she was sitting on the bare paving stones, with her back against the wall, surrounded by bulging carrier bags.

Serve you right for being in such a stupid place, Lee was going to yell. But he didn't, because he suddenly saw that she'd got hold of his shoe-bag.

When he fell, it had landed in her lap, and she was busy opening it and pulling out the shoes inside. All three pairs. When she looked up at Lee, her eyes were brighter than he had expected.

'Wotcher need three pairs for?' she said sharply. 'Only got one pair of feet, incher?' She waggled her own feet at him. They were fat and square and bursting out of their grubby, splitting trainers.

'They're not all *my* shoes,' Lee said.

'Stole them, didjer?' The bright eyes brightened even more.

'Of course not!' Lee snapped. 'I just didn't have time to put them away. I was being hustled, and – '

'Oh, *hustled*. I know all about that.' The old woman nodded sympathetically. 'You just get yourself settled out of the wind, and it's *Move on, Joyce. Can't sit there, Joyce. You're making the place untidy*.' She coughed – a thin, cracked cough – and pushed her fingers into one of Peanuts' trainers, feeling round the toes. 'Police, was it?'

'No!'

'OK. Keep your hair on.' Joyce spat on one of Fred's gleaming toecaps and rubbed off a mark with her filthy sleeve. 'Bin annoying yer teachers, have you?'

Lee was watching the shoes, trying to think of a way to snatch them back. He didn't mean to explain at all, but suddenly the words came bursting out.

'I was just tidying the shoes up for Miss Cherry – so that she wouldn't have to miss her badminton – and Mrs Puddock threw me out. Then Mr Merton sent me in again, and Mrs Puddock threw me out again and – '

His voice was getting faster and faster, and he stopped, before he lost control of it altogether. Joyce's eyes gleamed.

'Teachers!' she said, with relish. 'Don't never give you a chance to get yourself straight, do they? I could tell you a tale or two about teachers . . .'

The words disappeared into another cough and she picked up Lee's battered outdoor shoes, turning them over and over in her hands. For a moment, he thought she'd forgotten all about him. Then she looked up and grinned. Her teeth were the most horrible sight he had ever seen.

'Know what's wrong with teachers

like them? Hey?' She chuckled. 'They've forgotten what it's like. Oughter spend a day or two in your shoes, didn't they? That'd learn 'em all right.'

Lee nodded gloomily. 'It certainly would. I wish I could wave a magic wand and make it happen.'

'Pity you haven't got one.' Joyce's sharp, bright eyes flickered over his face. 'Want me to wave mine instead?'

She looked so solemn that Lee actually wondered whether she was serious. Then her face split into another disgusting grin and she started to laugh wheezily, bending over to clutch at her stomach.

'I'll split meself if I'm not careful. Gissa hand to get up, boy.'

She began to wallow about, struggling to lever herself off the ground. Her tattered cardigans bulged and gaped, as if she might pop out of them at any moment, and the zip of her skirt burst open, showing yards of bright pink petticoat. Lee wanted to run off and leave her, but he didn't see how she was ever going to get up if he did.

Gingerly, he reached out a hand towards her.

She grabbed it hard. 'That's it. *Heave!*'

Hauling on his arm, she lurched to her feet. But she couldn't keep hold of her carrier bags. They scattered everywhere and showers of rubbish cascaded across the coloured paving slabs. Bundles of rags and newspapers and teabags. A saucepan and some matches and a tangle of old stockings.

'There!' Joyce said, crossly. 'And now you'll run off, woncher? You'll cut and run, and I'll have ter pick up all me stuff meself.'

She bent over and began to scrabble

uselessly at the rubbish, puffing and panting.

'It's all right,' Lee said wearily. 'I'll help.'

He squatted down and scooped up handfuls of things, pushing them into the nearest bag without looking too closely at what he was touching. Joyce shuffled round behind him, reaching over to jam more things on top of the bags until they were ready to burst.

The moment Lee had picked everything up, she snatched the bags out of his hands. For the second time, her eyes flickered over his face. 'Ta very much. I won't forget I owe you a good turn.'

She shuffled off, faster than he had expected, but when she got to the entrance of the Arcade, she turned and grinned over her shoulder.

'Keep smiling. You never know what's going to happen tomorrow. Hey?'

With a wave of her carrier bags she was round the corner and into the street before Lee could say a word. He turned away and bent down to pick up his shoe-bag.

The moment he touched it, he knew there was something wrong. It looked full, but it was much too light. He wrenched it open – and pulled out handfuls of crumpled newspaper. There was nothing else inside. All three pairs of shoes had gone.

The thieving old –

'Hey!'

He raced to the entrance and flung himself out into the street. But Joyce was nowhere to be seen. She'd vanished completely. Slowly, Lee turned and began to walk back the other way. Now tomorrow was *sure* to be dreadful.

He'd never be able to write a poem about feet, so he'd be in trouble with Mr Merton.

He'd lost his outdoor shoes, so he'd be in trouble with Mrs Puddock.

And when Fred and Peanuts started fussing about their shoes, Miss Cherry was sure to ask him about them because he'd been the last person in the cloakroom. And he couldn't lie to *her*, so Fred and Peanuts would be out to get him too.

Dragging through the Arcade, he walked out at the other end into Birmingham Street. There was a sharp, cold wind blowing but he hardly noticed it. He was too busy worrying about what was going to happen the next day.

His life wouldn't be worth living.

3 *The Peculiar Boy*

Feet have very smelly toes.
Never put them near your nose.
Smelly socks will drive you mad
And athlete's foot is just as bad . . .

That was as far as Lee had got with his poem for Mr Merton. Every time he tried to go on, his mind went blank. Why should he bother with a stupid old poem when he was going to get into trouble anyway? If Mrs Puddock was raging about his lost shoes, and Fred and Peanuts were yelling at him, how could Mr Merton make things any worse?

If only he could stay at home and miss school! But his mother was already standing by the front door, calling impatiently.

'It's too late to fuss with that poem. Get your coat on. And you'll need your gloves and scarf too. It's *really* freezing today. Come on. If you don't go now, you'll be late.'

'But Mr Merton – '

'Mr Merton's ridiculous, giving you a poem like that to write. And you can tell him I said so.'

Honestly! Mothers! Lee pulled on his coat and rolled his eyes up at the ceiling. He could just imagine himself marching into school and going up to Mr Merton. *Hey, you! You're ridiculous! My mum says so.* That would really help, wouldn't it?

Wrapping the thick scarf three times round his neck, he picked up his bag and pushed the poem into it. Maybe he could make up the rest in his head and scribble it down when he got to school. If he didn't have to spend all the time dodging Fred and Peanuts.

Gloomily, he slouched out of the house and down the road, stamping in the frozen puddles and trying out lines in his head.

If your toenails get too long,
Cut them off before they pong –

No, that was silly.

If your toenails get too curly
They will think you are a girlie

And that was worse. He just couldn't concentrate while he was worrying about the lost shoes. What he really wanted was to get those back.

He began to walk faster, towards the Arcade. If Joyce was sitting in the same place as yesterday, he could grab hold of her and *make* her give the shoes back. Surely she'd be there. It was a good place to shelter from the wind. She *had* to be there.

But she wasn't.

Lee stood in the Arcade, looking up and down and peering into all the corners, but it was no use. There was no shabby figure sitting on the ground, or shuffling along, weighed down by carrier bags. The Arcade was completely empty except for a couple of early shoppers.

Sighing, he walked through and out at the other end into the High Street, stamping crossly on the thin ice that covered the puddles.

Peanuts and Fred. That was all he could think about. They were going to find out he'd lost their shoes, and they would – they would –

He couldn't bear to imagine it.

He barely noticed the person in front of him. He knew that there was someone just ahead and he walked slowly, on purpose, so that he wouldn't catch up, but he didn't look to see who it was.

Until a shrill voice said, 'You seem to be moving *very* slowly. Are you having trouble with your legs? Or is it your brain again?'

Lee looked up. He could hardly believe his eyes. 'You – what?'

The boy who'd spoken was no older than he was. And he was a complete stranger. Lee was sure of that, because he wasn't the sort of person anyone could forget.

He was so peculiar.

It was hard to work out why though.

Was it the long, navy-blue coat he was wearing? Or the satchel on his back? Or his old-fashioned striped cap? They were all quite plain and sensible, but each one of them was somehow – the wrong shape.

And his legs were bare.

On that freezing cold morning, with ice on the puddles and a cold north wind whipping round the corners of the buildings, the strange boy seemed to be wearing shorts. Between the bottom of his navy coat and the tops of his long grey socks, his spindly legs were blue with cold. Except at the back, where they were red and sore, chapped by the biting wind. Just looking at them made Lee want to shiver.

But if the boy was cold he wasn't taking any notice of it. He seemed much more interested in Lee. He looked sharply at him, beckoning with an impatient hand.

'Hurry up. Let's see you looking brisk.'

Brisk? Lee scowled at him. 'Brisk yourself,' he said rudely.

The boy's eyebrows went up so high that they vanished under his silly striped cap. He looked outraged. 'I hope I didn't hear what I thought I heard.'

Automatically, Lee bunched his fists. But he didn't really think the boy was looking for a fight. He sounded too cold and pompous for that, more like someone who wanted an apology. But that was ridiculous. An apology for what?

Lee stuck out his tongue. 'Wash your ears out!' he said.

He ran on ahead and, when he was a safe distance away, he turned round and called over his shoulder.

'And then go home and put your trousers on!'

The boy looked even more outraged. His eyes narrowed, his mouth tightened and he pulled himself up as if he were six feet tall. Silly idiot. Grinning, Lee ducked through the school gates, into the safety of the playground. Then he turned round to pull faces through the railings as the boy went past.

But he didn't go past. To Lee's amazement, he turned in at the gates and walked straight towards him. Quickly, Lee backed away towards the school building. Not that he was scared or anything – who could be scared of such a weird, skinny boy? – but there wasn't any point in looking for trouble.

The boy followed him.

Lee headed for the corner outside the Secretary's office window. If things turned really nasty, all he had to do was make a noise and Mrs Shepherd would come storming out.

The boy came straight towards him, looking solemn and determined, and Lee clenched his fists again. He wasn't going to start a fight, but he wasn't going to give in either. The moment there was any sign of a punch . . .

But it wasn't like that at all. The boy walked up to him, looked him up and down in a snooty way and then smiled again. A peculiar, tight smile.

'We've got a *lot* of things to sort out, haven't we?' he said coldly. 'Maybe you'd like a little time to think them all over. I'll see you outside the staff room, at the beginning of morning playtime.'

Lee was so amazed that he just stared. The boy didn't say anything else. He turned away abruptly and walked up to the front door of the school.

'Hey!' Lee began. 'We're not allowed–'

Then he stopped. Why should he help someone like that? If the boy didn't know the rules, he'd soon find out. And if he got into trouble, it would serve him right.

'I hope you get told off by Mrs Puddock,' Lee murmured. And then – because that was even worse – 'I hope you get your name in the Bad Book and *then* get told off by Mrs Puddock.'

If the strange boy heard, he didn't take any notice. He pushed the door open and tried to walk through it. But at exactly the same moment, Mr Willoughby came out with the bell. He was looking even more harassed and absent-minded than usual, but he wasn't so absent-minded that he didn't notice the boy trying to push past him into the building. He grabbed his shoulder.

'Can I help you?' he said mildly. 'I'm afraid you can't go inside yet.'

'What?' the boy said. He sounded surprised. Even annoyed. 'Of course I must go in. I'm late enough as it is.'

Mr Willoughby peered down at him, looking rather puzzled. 'You're not late. Especially not if you're new. What's your name?'

'Don't be ridiculous!' the boy snapped.

He tried to wriggle away from Mr Willoughby's clutching fingers, but it was no use. The fingers just gripped harder and Mr Willoughby pulled him away from the door, into the playground.

'I'm afraid there's no one in there to

look after you,' he said firmly. 'This is a rather difficult morning. If you wait until I've rung the bell, I'll sort you out then.'

Looking round, he spotted Lee, cowering under the window, and beckoned to him.

'Do us a favour, Lee. Things are a bit frantic today. Could you take care of – of – ' He peered down at the boy again. 'What is your name?'

A look of total disbelief spread across the strange boy's face. He half-closed his eyes. 'It's *me*, Geoffrey,' he said, very softly. 'Philip.'

At least, Lee *thought* that was what he said. But Mr Willoughby must have heard it differently. He smiled down and straightened the boy's striped cap. 'So you're called Geoffrey too, are you? Like me.' He nodded at Lee. 'Take care of Geoffrey Phillips, will you? I guess he'll probably be in your class. He looks about the right age.'

He strode off across the playground, getting ready to ring the bell. 'Geoffrey' stared after him, looking stunned. Then, as if he'd just thought of something, he glanced down at his own legs. Very carefully, he reached out a hand and touched one bare, chilly knee.

When he spoke to Lee, his voice was quite different from before. Shaky and uncertain.

'Do *you* think I look the right age for your class?'

'Around eleven?' Lee shrugged. 'Suppose so.'

Geoffrey's face went completely white, as though he'd had a terrible shock. He put out a hand to steady himself against the school wall and closed his eyes.

Lee was just going to ask him what the matter was, when he heard a loud, angry noise coming from the other side of the playground. He spun round, to find out what was happening.

And saw another stranger walking in through the gate.

4 *Disappearing Teachers*

A tall, fat girl was pushing her way through the crowd by the gate. She looked about the same age as Lee and Geoffrey, but she was twice as wide as either of them. Her coat strained tightly round her stomach and her hair was parted in the middle and dragged into two stringy plaits that hung down on either side of her red face.

She was yelling her head off.

'How about some MANNERS round here? Amy! William! Tom! Can't you see I'm trying to get through?'

No one liked that. Most of them pushed back, and the girl glared.

'Give me a bit of ROOM!' she bellowed.

Peanuts was turning cartwheels on the edge of the group. She spun the right way up and pulled a rude face.

'A *bit* of room? You need more than that.'

The girl's eyes almost popped out of her head and her face turned bright purple. But before she could yell again, Mr Willoughby rang the bell.

Nobody stopped, of course. Mr Willoughby usually had to ring two or three times before anyone took any notice. Everyone always ignored the first ring.

But Geoffrey didn't. To Lee's amazement, he froze. He snapped to attention like a soldier and stood staring straight at Mr Willoughby, waiting for him to speak.

The strange girl reacted to the bell as well, but she didn't stop moving. When she saw everyone racing about, she looked round impatiently with a frown. Then she knocked Peanuts out of her way and marched up to Mr Willoughby.

'Don't worry,' she whispered. 'I'll take over.'

At least, it was meant to be a whisper, but it was almost as loud as anyone else's shout and the words carried all over the playground. Mr Willoughby stared at her in bewilderment but she didn't seem to notice that. Reaching towards him, she snatched the bell out of his hands and rang it, hard.

And it worked – because everyone was so amazed.

All round the playground, people stopped dead in their tracks, waiting to see what would happen. The girl rang the bell again.

'RIGHT!' she yelled. 'GET INTO YOUR LINES!'

Mr Willoughby's mouth dropped open, but she didn't seem surprised.

'Don't dither around out here,' she hissed. 'Go inside and get on with something.'

That must have been the last straw. Mr Willoughby's neck turned bright red.

'Don't be silly!' he snapped. 'Give me that bell back!'

He grabbed at it, but the girl didn't let go. She clenched both hands round the handle, drew in her breath and pulled herself up very straight, glaring at him. For one glorious moment Lee thought they were going to have a fight.

Then Mr Willoughby tugged at the bell again, dragging the girl right up to him, so close that they were almost touching. He wasn't a tall man, but he was a lot taller than she was. Now they were so close, she had to tilt her head right back to go on glaring into his face.

Her head tilted – and as it went back her mouth fell open. She looked astonished to see him towering over her. Astonished and appalled.

Mr Willoughby seized his chance. 'That's not how we behave in this school,' he said firmly, twisting the bell out of her hands. 'Mrs Puddock is very keen on politeness. And she likes people to do what they're told, without arguing.' Then he smiled. He wasn't really stern. 'What's your name?'

The girl blinked up at him. 'I – er – Valerie P-P-P – '

Her mouth worked awkwardly, as if she was trying to force out a word that wouldn't come. Peanuts nudged Fred.

'Doesn't even know her own name,' she whispered. Her whisper was just as loud as Valerie's and, all round the playground, people started to giggle.

Valerie glared at her, took a deep breath and made an enormous effort to speak. 'Valerie – P-Pilkington.'

She blinked. As if she'd surprised herself.

Mr Willoughby waved a hand across the playground at Peanuts. 'Pauline! Come and look after Valerie, will you?'

'Me?' Peanuts said. Lee could see her getting ready to argue. Then she looked at Mr Willoughby again. His neck was still dangerously pink. 'OK,' she said. 'Over here, Val.'

Valerie hesitated, looking back at Mr Willoughby.

'Oh, come *on*,' Peanuts said, impatiently. She strode across the playground and caught hold of Valerie's arm. Then she smiled kindly at Mr Willoughby. 'Would you like us to get into lines?'

'Oh. Yes,' Mr Willoughby said. As if he'd only just remembered about the lines.

He rang the bell again, in a vague way, and waited while people shuffled about. Lee looked round for Geoffrey, to tell him where to line up.

But Geoffrey was already there.

He was standing in exactly the right place, where Miss Cherry's class always lined up. Standing stiffly to attention, at the very front of the line, with his head up and his arms by his sides. Lee felt a strange shiver run up his spine.

How had he known where to go?

Lee slid into place behind him, and Peanuts dragged Valerie up into the next place. Then they all waited for Mr Willoughby to ring the bell again and send them inside.

But he didn't. Instead, he raised his

voice and shouted across the playground. 'Listen, everyone. When you've hung up your coats, I want you to go straight into the Hall for Assembly.'

'But it's *Tuesday*,' Fred said. He liked putting people right. Especially teachers. 'We don't have Assembly on Tuesday morning, sir.'

'Well, you're having it this morning!' Mr Willoughby snapped. He rubbed a hand across his forehead and lowered his voice. 'This morning is a bit special. We're rather short of teachers and – '

That was a silly way to start. The rest of his sentence was drowned by loud cheers from all over the playground. He flapped his hand to make people be quiet, but the cheers just got louder.

'For goodness' SAKE!' said a loud voice behind Lee. 'Why don't you all LISTEN? The behaviour in this playground is APPALLING!'

It was Valerie. Peanuts turned round and glared at her. 'Oh sorr-*ee*. Pardon me for living.'

Valerie snorted, and Lee caught his breath. Hadn't she got any sense?

Couldn't she see she was heading for trouble?

Mr Willoughby cleared his throat and spoke above the remains of the cheering. 'As I said, three members of staff are unexpectedly – er – delayed and – '

Some people started cheering again, but Fred stopped them this time. 'Shut up, you lot,' he hissed. 'Don't you *want* to know who isn't here?' He smiled winningly at Mr Willoughby. His Model Pupil smile. 'Who is it, sir?'

Mr Willoughby looked cautiously at them. 'At the *moment*, we're waiting for Miss Cherry – '

No cheers for that. But Lee closed his eyes for a moment, in relief. If Miss Cherry was away, Peanuts and Fred wouldn't be able to find out who'd lost their shoes.

' – and Mr Merton – ' Mr Willoughby said.

There were loud cheers from Mr Merton's class.

' – and – er – Mrs Puddock.'

This time there were mammoth, enormous cheers. Mr Willoughby rang the bell as loudly as he could, but it was completely impossible to hear. It was only when the cheering started to die down that Lee heard Valerie muttering behind him.

' . . . terrible behaviour! And anyway, *I'm* not away – '

She didn't get any further because Peanuts grabbed hold of her and jammed a hand over her mouth. 'For goodness' SAKE!' she said with relish. 'Why don't you LISTEN? The behaviour in this playground is APPALLING!'

Valerie gurgled furiously under the gagging hand, but no one took any notice of her. They were all shouting questions at Mr Willoughby.

'Why are they all off, sir?'

'What are they doing?'

'Who's going to teach us?'

Mr Willoughby yelled above the noise. 'Don't worry. There'll be other teachers here in a little while. You'll be all right.'

'How can three teachers disappear at once?' That was Fred, of course. He always asked the most awkward questions. 'Where *are* they?'

Mr Willoughby sighed. 'We don't *know* where they are.'

That was it. The whole playground went wild.

'They've stolen all the money and gone to Spain!'

'Someone's kidnapped them! There's going to be a ransom demand!'

'They've all been *murdered*!'

It was chaos. In the end, Mr Willoughby gave up and pointed at the door and everyone headed into school at the same time, pushing and shoving. Lee looked round for Geoffrey, to show him the way to the cloakroom – but Geoffrey was already ahead. By the time Lee caught up with him, he was hanging his coat on the empty peg.

Lee stood looking at him, trying not to shiver. Geoffrey knew everything without being told. It was spooky. And now that he'd taken his coat off, he looked even more peculiar. Long baggy shorts, down to his knees. A scruffy blazer with a pullover underneath. And hair that was long on top but very, very short at the back and sides. He reminded Lee of something. For a moment he couldn't place it, and then it came to him.

Grandpa.

He looked exactly like the school photos of Lee's grandfather. Scrawny and awkward, with baggy clothes. No one wore clothes quite like that now. Everything was wrong. From his head right down –

Lee glanced down, to check his shoes – and that was the weirdest thing of all. Because they *weren't* wrong. They were the most familiar shoes in the whole world. Shabby and scuffed, with a long, deep scratch across the left toe.

Geoffrey was wearing *his* shoes. The ones that Joyce had run away with.

5 *What Are You Doing in My Shoes?*

For a second, Lee was totally stunned. Motionless. He couldn't do anything except stare down at Geoffrey's feet, with Joyce's words ringing in his head.

Know what's wrong with teachers like them? They've forgotten what it's like. Oughter spend a day or two in your shoes, didn't they? . . . I won't forget I owe you a good turn . . .

And now here was Geoffrey. In his shoes. 'Geoffrey Phillips' was Mr Merton. Philip Merton.

But – that was impossible. Wasn't it?

Lee went on staring down at the shoes, trying to get up enough courage to look Geoffrey in the face. But before he managed it, there was a furious bellow from Peanuts.

'Who's had my shoes? Come on! One of you's nicked my shoes!'

A second later, Fred yelled from the other side of the cloakroom. 'And what about mine?'

Lee kept his head down. They wouldn't guess he had anything to do with it. Not if he kept quiet. But his brain was working fast. *Shoes again.*

His eyes slid sideways to the girls' side of the cloakroom. Valerie was hanging her coat next to Peanuts' purple anorak, and her feet were planted firmly on the ground opposite Lee.

She was wearing Fred's shoes.

There was no mistake. They were Fred's shiny lace-ups, with a faint dull mark on the left toe, where Joyce had spat on it and rubbed it dry with her sleeve. And Valerie looked just as peculiar as Geoffrey. No one else had a pinafore dress like hers. Or hair wrenched into tight plaits, as if the person who'd done them was trying to pull the hair right out at the roots.

Valerie was Mrs Puddock.

Lee started grinning. It was wonderful. Mr Merton and Mrs Puddock were eleven years old again. *Now* they'd find

out what it was really like! They'd
see –

Suddenly Geoffrey turned away from
his peg, smoothing a hand over his hair.
And he caught sight of Lee's grin. He
glanced round the cloakroom to see
what was so funny, but there was no
obvious joke and he looked back at Lee,
with his eyebrows raised.

Like someone asking a question.

No! Lee gulped and bent down
quickly, pretending to tie his shoe.
Geoffrey mustn't guess that he knew
anything about the change. That would
be disastrous.

Peanuts and Fred were steaming
through the cloakroom, looking for their
shoes. They kept tipping all the things
out of shoe-bags and rummaging
around on the floor, but they didn't take
any notice of what people were wearing.
Fred actually pushed Valerie out of the
way as he crawled under the bench
behind her, but he didn't even glance at
her feet.

By the time Mr Willoughby walked
into the cloakroom, there were a lot of

grumbling people. 'Hurry *up*!' Mr Willoughby said, impatiently. 'Things are difficult enough this morning, without fussing.'

Peanuts looked injured. 'But I can't find my indoor shoes.'

'Wear your outdoor shoes then, you silly girl! Just get into the Hall. We're going to have a hymn practice.'

He began to hustle people, and everyone started surging forward, jamming the corridor. Fred elbowed his way through the crowd, shoving Geoffrey back against the pegs.

'Dear me,' Geoffrey said, in his funny, dry voice. 'You *are* keen on hymn practice, aren't you?'

Fred snorted and gave another shove so that the pegs dug into Geoffrey's back. '*You* can be late if you like. I'm not going to risk it. Old Wally Willoughby's in enough of a state already.'

He gave Geoffrey a third shove, for luck, and began to push his way along the corridor. Geoffrey peeled himself off the pegs and brushed fussily at the sleeves of his blazer. Then he, too, set off down the corridor, muttering as he edged past people.

'Excuse me, please. Excuse me, please. Excuse me.'

It was all Lee could do not to giggle out loud as he followed him into the Hall. But the grin didn't last long because the hymn practice was even worse than usual. With Miss Cherry away, there was no one to play the piano. Mr Willoughby boomed out all the tunes in his deep, wobbly voice, flapping his hands to tell everyone to join in. And the more he sang, the more agitated he seemed. He kept looking nervously towards the double doors at the back of the hall.

Lee guessed that he was waiting for more teachers to arrive so that he could finish the hymn practice. But the doors stayed firmly shut, all through 'Morning has broken' and 'What shall we do with our lives this morning?' and into 'Little drops of water'.

Everyone else was beginning to get restless too. Especially Geoffrey and Valerie. Geoffrey's fingers tapped irritably against the chair in front and Valerie kept sighing under her breath.

'This is RIDICULOUS,' she was muttering. 'Why doesn't the man get a GRIP on things?'

Mr Willoughby pulled out a large white handkerchief and mopped his forehead. 'Now, let's have a go at – '

And then the doors did open.

'You sound as if you could do with a bit of help,' said a bright, silvery voice.

For a split second, hope lit up Mr Willoughby's eyes. Then he looked down the Hall at the figure coming through the doors, and his expression changed, to one of bewilderment.

It was a girl of about eleven. Another new girl. But she didn't look like anyone Lee had ever seen at school before. She was small and slight, with huge blue eyes, and she seemed to be wearing some kind of fancy dress. Long, grubby, fair hair drizzled down her back, trailing over a very odd assortment of clothes.

Her dress was made of cream lace, with a green silk jerkin over the top. And over that was a red velvet jacket, with a gold dragon on one sleeve. She looked like a ragamuffin princess out of some fairy-tale.

As soon as they saw her, people began to whisper, but that didn't seem to worry her. She padded up the Hall, smiling at Mr Willoughby and fluttering her eyelashes.

'I'm sorry I'm so late. I just *couldn't* start the car, so I had to walk all the way—'

'Yes — well — um — ' Mr Willoughby looked even more bewildered. 'I hope you've got a note from your mother.'

For some reason, the girl seemed to find that hysterically funny. She let out a great shriek of laughter. 'I should have asked her for one, shouldn't I?'

Mr Willoughby was looking very rattled now, as if he couldn't cope with any more problems. 'You need a note from *someone*,' he said severely.

The girl looked startled, but she didn't say anything. Instead, she walked straight up to the piano and sat down on the stool. 'Let's get on with the hymn practice, shall we? What were you singing? "Little drops of water"?'

Raising her hands above the keys, she smiled at Mr Willoughby and brought them down confidently, as if she were launching into the tune. But it wasn't the tune that she played. It was a huge, crashing discord.

The noise seemed to stun her. For a second, she just stared down at her fingers, as though she couldn't believe what they had done. Then she gave a silly little laugh.

'Oh dear! I'd better try again, hadn't I?' Lifting one hand, she patted at her tangled hair, glancing sideways as she

did so to see her reflection in the window.

No! Lee thought. *It can't be*! That funny little hair-patting gesture was exactly what Miss Cherry did whenever she made a silly mistake. She patted her hair and looked at her pretty, neat reflection, as if it gave her confidence.

But when the ragamuffin girl looked sideways she didn't see the pretty, neat reflection of a grown-up woman. She saw a grubby little girl in peculiar clothes. And she froze, with one hand still on her hair, staring at the window, as though she couldn't believe her eyes.

Lee couldn't believe it either. What was going on? Miss Cherry wasn't mean and bad-tempered. She never told people off, except when she had to, because of Mrs Puddock and Mr Merton. Why had *she* gone back to being eleven?

Mr Willoughby cleared his throat. 'Maybe we ought to start again. Properly. What's your name?'

The girl swallowed. 'Mar – Marigold.' Her voice was very, very faint, but her eyes were sharp and bright. Lee could see that she was working out what to do.

Mr Willoughby gave her a patient smile. 'Well, Marigold, you'd better sit down with the others for a moment or two. I'm just going to send everyone out into the playground.'

As if she were in a dream, Marigold stood up and padded down the Hall to the empty seat beside Lee. Without even glancing at him, she sat back in the chair, closing her eyes.

Mr Willoughby wiped his forehead with his big white handkerchief. 'All right now,' he said in a voice that croaked from too much singing. 'Lead out in rows from the back. *Quietly*.'

Everyone stood up at once, turned round and started to push. Lee was near the front of the crowd, with Marigold just ahead of him, and they had almost reached the door when there was a loud yell from behind.

'What are you doing in my shoes?'

Marigold looked down at her feet, as if she were seeing the shoes for the first time. She frowned a tiny, delicate frown. 'I don't know – '

'They're *my* shoes!' Peanuts said. She gave a fierce shove, trying to push past the people in between them.

Marigold stood steady for a moment. 'Look, why don't you calm down and – ?'

Peanuts gave a great roar of rage. '*Calm down*? You little – '

For one second more, Marigold stood very straight. Then she saw it wasn't going to have any effect. Her eyes widened and she turned and ran out of the Hall and down the corridor, with the big, loose trainers smacking on the floor.

By the time Lee caught up with them, they were in the playground. Peanuts had pinned Marigold to the ground and she was busy wrenching at the trainers.

'Don't know – how you got them – ' she was panting furiously, 'but they're – *mine*!'

Marigold lay there on the tarmac, gazing up pathetically.

'Poor little thing,' Fred muttered. He was right behind Lee. 'She's terrified.' He went sailing in and grabbed Peanuts' arm just as she was about to pull the first trainer off Marigold's foot. 'Why don't you pick on someone your own size? She hasn't even got any socks on, and it's *freezing*.'

Peanuts sniffed. 'If she's daft enough to come to school without shoes and socks, she deserves to freeze.'

'It's not my fault,' Marigold said, in a small, sad voice. 'My mother thinks feet ought to grow naturally. To reach their true beauty.'

There was a loud snort from Valerie, at the back of the crowd. 'True beauty? That's the sort of rubbish people used to talk in the nineteen sixties. What *you* need is a good pair of tights – and proper school uniform.'

Lee wanted to shake her. It wasn't Miss Cherry's fault if she'd been eleven in the nineteen sixties. Why was Valerie being so mean? Did she think everyone had to be the same as she was?

Marigold's mouth trembled miserably. 'Oh, I'd like school uniform. I really would. But my father says it's wicked to make people conform. They have to be free to develop in their own way. If they all wear the same clothes, it stunts their individuality.'

Valerie snorted again and Fred spun round furiously, letting go of Peanuts' hands.

'It's a pity *your* parents don't care more about true beauty. If they did, you wouldn't look like a stale bread pudding.'

Valerie spluttered. 'You – you – !'

But no one took any notice of what she was saying – because Peanuts had seized her chance. The moment Fred let go of her hands, she lunged forward and grabbed at Marigold's feet again. Tugging at the trainers, she pulled them off, one after the other.

Then she sat back on her heels. 'Right!' she said fiercely. 'I left these in the cloakroom yesterday. I know I did. So there's something *very peculiar* going on. Who took them out of school and gave them to you?'

Marigold sat up and blinked at the shoes. 'Took them out of school?' she said, slowly.

Lee didn't want her to remember the shoe mountain. He stepped back, out of sight – but that was a mistake. He'd hidden from Marigold, but someone else had noticed his quick, guilty movement. When he glanced round, he saw Geoffrey watching him.

With a thoughtful expression on his face.

6 *A Terrible Way to Talk to a Teacher!*

For one dreadful moment, Lee thought Geoffrey was actually going to start asking questions. But Fred stopped that. He came sailing in to rescue Marigold again and gave Peanuts a great shove that pushed her over sideways, against Geoffrey's legs. Geoffrey went staggering backwards against the wall.

Fred grabbed Marigold's hand. 'Don't take any notice of Peanuts,' he said scornfully. 'She's just a bully. You don't want to wear anything that's been on *her* feet, do you? Come and get some shoes out of the secondhand uniform cupboard instead.'

He pulled Marigold up and led her away, leaving Peanuts sprawled on the ground with her mouth open. For a second, she lay there looking hurt. Then she sat up and tossed her head.

'Don't know why you're all standing around,' she muttered defiantly. 'This is playtime, isn't it? We ought to be playing football.'

'Playing football is against the rules,' Geoffrey said stiffly, from the wall. 'As you very well know.'

Peanuts tossed her head again. 'Who cares about rules? Old Merton's away, and Wally Willoughby won't tell us off. I'm going to sneak a football out of the games cupboard.'

She bounced into school and came out a second later with a ball under her arm.

'Here! Lee!'

As she kicked it towards him, Lee realised what they were going to do. It was brilliant. They were going to play football right under Geoffrey's nose. Right under *Mr Merton's* nose. And he wouldn't be able to do a thing about it.

Lee booted the ball back, enjoying that kick more than any other kick in his whole life. Then he turned round to enjoy the fury on Geoffrey's face.

But he had a shock. Because Geoffrey

wasn't looking at them. He was sitting on the bench at the side of the playground, still looking thoughtful. And he was taking off his left shoe.

No! Lee thought again. He mustn't take that shoe off! Because, if he did, he'd find the name written on the inside of the tongue. *Lee Godwin*. He had to be stopped.

Lee called out the first thing that came into his head. 'Why are you taking your shoes off? Aren't you coming to play football?'

'I – was looking for a stone,' Geoffrey muttered. Quickly, he slipped his foot back into the shoe.

Lee pointed into the middle of the playground. 'So? Are you coming to play?'

'I – ' A strange expression flitted across Geoffrey's face. Then he folded his lips primly. 'Of course not. It's against the rules.' But he seemed to have forgotten about the shoes. Standing up, he sauntered across the playground to lean against the railings.

Lee raced off after the ball, but he

found it hard to concentrate on the game. He kept glancing round nervously, to see what Geoffrey was doing.

It was all right though. Because Geoffrey stood perfectly still for the rest of break, staring at the football as it zigzagged across the playground.

Watching every kick.

Mr Willoughby gave them a quarter of an hour and then came to call them in. He didn't waste time trying to get people into lines. He just swung the bell, hard, and pointed at the school and everyone raced for the doors.

'Who d'you think we've got?' Peanuts muttered to Lee as they went down the corridor to their classroom. 'D'you think Miss Cherry's back?'

'I – um – ' Lee glanced at Marigold, who was walking demurely ahead of them. 'No, I don't think so. It must be someone else.'

'Bet I know who,' Fred said gloomily. 'Who do we *always* get?' He reached the classroom door, stuck his head round and then turned back, pulling a face. 'Told you so.'

Sitting at the front of the class was a familiar, large, grey-haired figure. Mrs Puddock's best friend.

Lee pulled a face too. 'Mrs Hemingway!' he muttered.

Everyone behind him groaned – except for Valerie. The moment she heard the name 'Hemingway', her face lit up.

'Let me through!' she said loudly. 'Get out of my WAY!'

She started pushing at people and jabbing with her elbows until she was at the front of the crowd. Then she marched across the classroom and leaned forward, with her hands on the teacher's desk, to whisper to Mrs Hemingway.

And her whisper, of course, carried right to the door.

'Mildred, you've got to help. It's me. Valerie.'

Slowly, Mrs Hemingway lifted her head. Pursing her lips, she folded up her knitting with a frown and shook her head at Valerie. 'Now now, dear. I don't know what they did at your last school, but we don't call teachers by their Christian names here.'

Valerie banged her hand impatiently on the table. 'But it's me!'

'Of course it's you,' Mrs Hemingway said. 'You couldn't be somebody else, could you now?' She gave a silly little laugh.

'IT'S ME!' Valerie grabbed at the front of her cardigan and shook it hard. 'You've got to listen, Mildred – '

Mrs Hemingway stopped smiling and

her eyes narrowed. 'Got to? That's a terrible way to talk to a teacher. Let go at once, you naughty girl!'

'I'm not a naughty girl! I'm – '

'Let *go!*' Mrs Hemingway smacked Valerie's hands hard, one after the other. Then she pulled them off her cardigan and stood up, dragging Valerie away from her desk. 'If you don't start behaving properly, you're going to be in trouble.'

She pushed Valerie into an empty seat, between Peanuts and Marigold, and stepped back, brushing off her hands.

'Sit there and be quiet!'

Valerie slumped sulkily into the chair without saying a word, but the space wasn't really big enough for her. Peanuts wriggled and tried to push her sideways.

'There isn't *room* for six people here, Mrs Hemingway. Not if one of them's Valerie.'

Mrs Hemingway shrugged. 'Just sit quietly, dear, and everything will be fine. Now take out your language books and write about what you did at the weekend.'

Lee groaned and Fred pulled a face. Wearily, they took out their pens and found their language books. Geoffrey sat down in between them and stuck up his hand.

'I haven't got a language book.'

'Then use some rough paper,' Mrs Hemingway said impatiently. 'Goodness, haven't you got any initiative?'

Geoffrey stared at her for a moment, but he didn't say another word. He just got up, walked straight over to the rough paper tray and took out a bundle of paper. Then he chose three pencils out of the spare pencil tin and went across to Marigold and Valerie, to give them some pencils and paper too.

Lee glanced round to see if anyone noticed how odd that was, but all the others were busy trying to remember what had happened at the weekend. Peanuts was scribbling hard already and Fred was making notes down the side of his paper. He liked to get everything in order before he began to write.

Only Valerie and Marigold, with their sheets of rough paper, seemed to be having trouble. Valerie was staring at the paper as though she hadn't an idea in her head, and Marigold was frowning and chewing the end of her pencil.

Hah! Lee thought, triumphantly. Served them right! They were always telling children to sit down and write things. Now they'd find out how difficult it was sometimes.

He wasn't stuck today though. He had plenty to write about. As Mrs Hemingway glanced towards him, he seized his pencil and began.

On Saturday, my dad bought me a new game for my computer. It is ACE. I scored 2340 before lunch and I'm up to the third level now. Some of the bosses are really hard to beat . . .

He leaned closer to the paper, forgetting everyone else for a moment. NIGHT

RAIDERS was a brilliant game and he could go on about it for hours. But he'd only reached the bottom of the first page when a ball of screwed-up paper flicked him on the nose. He looked up and saw Fred grinning at him, with his finger on his lips.

What was that for? Lee mouthed.

Fred didn't answer. Not in words, anyway. Instead, he grinned and pointed at Geoffrey, who was scribbling away next to him. And at Geoffrey's paper. The sheet was half-covered with writing now. Not Mr Merton's tiny, cramped script, but a different kind of writing altogether. Round and childish, with loops on all the letters. Lee leaned in closer and read the words.

On Saturday morning I had a shower and a shave. Then I read the Financial Times *for half an hour before I went out to do my shopping. After the shopping, I called in at the Dog and Duck for a quick pint of beer . . .*

A pint of beer? Lee started to giggle. Whatever was Mrs Hemingway going to say when she read that?

They didn't have to wait long to find out. She happened to glance up from her knitting just then and she saw Lee giggling. Hauling herself to her feet, she lumbered across the classroom to see what had made him laugh.

The moment she saw Geoffrey's work, she frowned like thunder. 'You *naughty* little boy!' She grabbed his sleeve and hauled him to his feet. 'How dare you be so impertinent!'

Geoffrey stood very stiff and still. Like a block of ice. 'You told us to write about what we did at the weekend.'

'And you want me to believe that you read the *Financial Times* and went to a pub?' Mrs Hemingway shook his shoulder. 'No! Don't say another word! You can just take your chair and go and sit outside in the corridor. And you can write a proper piece of work while you're out there.'

She screwed up his paper and tossed it towards the rubbish bin. Then she stood with her hands on her hips, watching Geoffrey carry his chair to the door.

He didn't hurry. He walked slowly and steadily past all the tables, with his chair in one hand and his pencil and paper in the other. As he stepped out into the corridor, he turned round suddenly.

'You don't care what I did at the weekend,' he said in a cold, angry voice. 'You were just too lazy to think of anything else for us to do. If you were a good teacher, you wouldn't be telling me off. You'd be wondering why I wrote something so peculiar.'

'If — ? How dare you!' Mrs Hemingway began to march across the classroom towards him.

Geoffrey didn't give up. He just talked faster and faster to fit in what he wanted to say before she reached him. 'I'll tell you why I wrote it. I was testing you. I don't believe you were even going to read what we wrote. You were just making us write it to fill up the time. If Lee hadn't laughed, you would never even have looked at what I wrote. I can't *bear* teachers who waste children's time.'

Mrs Hemingway had reached him now. She towered over him, glaring, but she didn't shout. She just said, 'Well! That's not very nice, is it, dear?'

Then she jammed one hand over his mouth, crashed his chair down with the other, just outside the door, and pushed Geoffrey into it. She pushed so hard that the chair skidded backwards and he banged his head on the wall.

'That's better,' she said comfortably. 'Now you sit there until you've done two pages of *sensible* writing.' She walked back into the classroom and looked round. 'How are the rest of you getting on?'

Everybody nodded and scribbled hard, trying not to attract her attention. Even Peanuts, who was still squashed up on the front table, seemed to have stopped wriggling and resigned herself to sitting with her elbows glued to her sides. Mrs Hemingway beamed and waddled back to her chair.

'Very good. Now let's all get some work done.'

Everyone nodded meekly and began to scribble. Except Lee. He found himself glancing sideways at the doorway to where Geoffrey was bent over his paper.

I can't bear *teachers who waste children's time*. That had sounded as if he really cared what children did.

Suddenly, Lee felt uncomfortable. He didn't *want* to be sorry for Geoffrey. Geoffrey was dangerous. He thought too much.

Picking up his pencil, Lee tried to force his mind back to NIGHT RAIDERS. But it was very hard. He kept glancing round to make sure that Geoffrey's shoes were still safely on his feet. And that Geoffrey was concentrating on his writing.

Finally he managed to think up another sentence, but he had only written half of it when he was disturbed again. There was a little squeak from the front table and, with a loud crash, Marigold's chair went flying sideways, sending her sprawling on the floor.

7 *The Bad Book*

Anyone else would have made a fuss and shouted at the person who'd pushed the chair over. But Marigold didn't say a word. She just sat up and rubbed her elbow pathetically, looking up with big, reproachful eyes.

At Valerie.

Those big blue eyes were much more effective. After one glimpse of them, Mrs Hemingway came storming over.

'That wasn't very nice, Valerie! I told you you'd be in trouble if you didn't behave yourself.'

Valerie looked astounded. 'But I didn't do a thing! She – '

'Now then!' Mrs Hemingway's voice grew sharper. 'I hope you're not trying to tell me that poor little Marigold knocked her own chair over. And threw herself onto the floor.'

'Well – ' Valerie blinked and went pink. 'Well – yes, she did, actually.'

She sounded as if she could hardly believe it herself. As if she didn't expect anyone else to believe her either. Lee could see why. She was so large and angry and Marigold was so small and frail that it seemed obvious who'd done the pushing. After all, Valerie had grabbed Mrs Hemingway, hadn't she?

There was an angry rumble from Fred. 'What a bully!' He glared at Valerie and then gave Marigold a sympathetic smile.

So did Mrs Hemingway. 'Well, dear? What have you got to say? Did you push your own chair over and throw yourself onto the floor?' Her voice showed that she thought the whole idea was ridiculous.

'I – ' Marigold rubbed her elbow again, but she didn't contradict Mrs Hemingway. She just looked at Valerie with her bottom lip trembling. 'I think I must have been in the way,' she said faintly. 'I don't suppose Valerie could help pushing – '

'But I *didn't* push!' Valerie's face was

scarlet now 'You just – '

'That's enough!' Mrs Hemingway snapped. 'Pick your chair up and sit down again, Marigold. Valerie will have to go somewhere else.'

With her eyes lowered demurely, Marigold turned her chair the right way up and slipped into her place.

Until that moment, Lee had assumed that Mrs Hemingway was right and that Valerie had done the pushing. Mrs Puddock was always pushing people. But as Marigold settled herself back in her chair, she spread her work into Valerie's space and wriggled her shoulders.

There was something smug about that wriggle. Something that didn't quite fit the poor-little-Marigold picture. She looked like a cat that had got the place it wanted, beside the fire.

Lee suddenly wondered who *had* knocked the chair over.

Mrs Hemingway obviously had no doubts. She looked at Valerie with distaste. 'Right. Now I'll deal with you.'

'Listen,' Valerie said, stubbornly. '*I*

didn't push her over. She did it herself.'

Mrs Hemingway pressed her lips together. 'We don't like liars in this school, Valerie. That's something you're going to have to learn, I can see.'

Valerie put her head up, defiantly. 'I'm not a liar!' She hesitated and then plunged on, as if she couldn't stop the words coming out. 'You always were a stubborn, self-opinionated woman, Mildred!'

There was a gasp from the rest of the class and Mrs Hemingway's face went pale with fury. 'Maybe I won't deal with you myself after all,' she said slowly. 'I think I'll let Mrs Puddock sort you out instead. When she gets back to school.'

Mrs Puddock? For a moment, Lee felt like laughing. Then he looked at Valerie's face and he wasn't quite so sure. She'd gone bright red and her lips were pinched together as if she were trying to stop more words bursting out. She obviously didn't like being told off any more than any of them did.

The others were all watching Mrs Hemingway with their mouths open.

Because they'd guessed what she was going to say next. She let them wait a moment. Lee almost had the feeling that she was enjoying the suspense.

Then she said very solemnly, 'Valerie – do you know where the Secretary's office is?'

'Yes,' Valerie said sulkily.

'Go there, then. Ask for the Bad Book, and bring it back here to me.'

There was a buzz of muttering round the class. Having your name in the Bad Book meant that what you had done was too awful for an ordinary teacher to sort out. It had to be saved up for Mrs Puddock.

Only Peanuts, in their class, had ever had her name in the Bad Book. Lee didn't know what had happened when she finally saw Mrs Puddock, because she wouldn't say, but afterwards she had been very, very careful what she did. For a whole term.

As Valerie walked out of the class, everyone's head turned to follow her. She held herself defiantly straight but her face was very red. And it went red again when she came back into the room and everyone looked at the book in her hand.

It wasn't very big – just a medium-sized blue notebook – but every eye in the class was fixed on it as she walked down the class and dropped it on the desk in front of Mrs Hemingway.

Mrs Hemingway picked it up and leafed through, looking for the first clean page. Then she picked up a pen to write Valerie's name in the book.

'You don't do that first,' Peanuts said, half under her breath. 'You – ' Then she stopped.

Mrs Hemingway looked up. 'What, dear?'

But it was Valerie who answered. 'There's a message at the front of the book,' she said stiffly. 'From Mrs Puddock. You're supposed to read it out to me. Shall I tell you what it says?'

Without waiting for an answer, she began to recite, in a sharp, harsh voice. *'Your name is going to be written in this book because you have been VERY BADLY-BEHAVED. If I were at school myself, I should deal with you STRAIGHT AWAY.'*

Mrs Hemingway looked startled.

So did Peanuts. 'That's weird,' she whispered to Marigold. 'That's *exactly* what it says. She must have learnt the words while she was bringing the book back here.'

But it wasn't just the words. It was the way Valerie said them. Fred nudged Lee.

'Here!' he whispered. 'She sounds just like Mrs Puddock. But she's never even seen her. How does she *know*?'

'Maybe – maybe she *is* Mrs Puddock,' Lee said daringly. 'In disguise.'

Fred didn't believe him. He just thought it was a joke, and he grinned and punched Lee's arm because Valerie said the next word in precisely the way Mrs Puddock would have done.

'UnFORTunately, I'm not at school today. So your name will be written down and when I return I shall call you to my office IMMEDIATELY. Until then, think about what you have done, until you understand why your teacher is so ANGRY with you.'

It was like a mad dream. There was Mrs Puddock telling herself off – and Lee hadn't got anyone to share it with. Even if he tried to tell the rest of the class they wouldn't listen. No one could believe it except him. No one, in a million years, would believe that a teacher could change into one of the schoolchildren.

Except –

Suddenly, he realised that he was wrong. And all at once it wasn't so funny any more. There were two other people who *knew* that things like that could happen, and they were both listening to Valerie. They'd probably guessed who she was by now.

He let his eyes slide sideways towards the table where Marigold was sitting.

Everyone else there was staring at Valerie, and most of them were trying not to grin, but Marigold wasn't grinning. She'd taken the opportunity of spreading her papers even further across the table and she seemed to be drawing an intricate, complicated picture at the bottom of the writing she'd done.

It's all right, Lee thought, with relief. *She hasn't got a clue. She thinks she's the only person who's changed*. He could hardly believe it, but it was obvious. Now that Marigold had got rid of Valerie, she just wasn't interested in her.

Very slowly, so that no one would notice, he turned his head the other way, towards the door. And suddenly he felt quite sick. Geoffrey was peering round the door – and his face was quite different from Marigold's.

He knew all right.

Lee swallowed. Geoffrey was gazing at Valerie as if he couldn't believe what he was hearing. Looking sympathetic and horrified and – confused. He knew who she was.

Lee looked away quickly before Geoffrey caught him watching. His heart was thudding fast. What would happen when those two got talking? Would they compare notes? Compare *shoes?* It wouldn't take them long to work out that he'd got something to do with what had happened.

What could he do?

'*I'll see you when I get back,*' Valerie said loudly, finishing her recitation from the Bad Book. '*IMMEDIATELY.*'

Mrs Hemingway nodded briskly. She hadn't noticed anything at all. Valerie obviously didn't remind *her* of Mrs Puddock.

'If you've gone to the trouble to learn all that, I hope you've taken it to heart.' Flipping through the book, she found the first clean page and wrote Valerie's name on it. Then she snapped the book shut. 'There. Now take it back to the Secretary.'

Valerie stomped sulkily across the classroom. Geoffrey was still in the doorway, waiting for her. As she reached him, he leaned close to her ear. His voice was very soft, but Lee was listening desperately and he caught the words.

'We've got to talk – '

He might just as well have spoken to a statue. Valerie went straight past him with her face blank and her head held high. He might have guessed who she was, but she obviously had no idea about him. She just ignored him.

Fred didn't though. He hadn't heard what Geoffrey said, but he'd seen him whispering and that was enough. He prodded Lee with a sharp finger.

'See that?'

'See what?' Lee said cautiously.

Fred grinned and jerked his head backwards at the doorway to where Geoffrey was sitting. Then he scribbled on the edge of a piece of rough paper.

Geoffrey 4 Valerie

With a smirk, he began to fold the piece of paper into a dart. When Mrs Hemingway wasn't looking, he launched the dart across the classroom.

It hit Peanuts on the back of the head and fell behind her chair.

With a swift, practised movement, Peanuts knocked her book onto the floor. Catching her breath, as if she were annoyed with herself, she pushed her chair back, bent down and scooped up both the book and the paper dart so quickly that Mrs Hemingway didn't notice what she was doing.

She was so used to reading notes in class that Lee didn't even see her do it, but he knew when she had got the message. She glanced quickly over her shoulder and gave Fred a wicked grin.

Lee wished he could join in the joke. But he knew better. If he'd been writing notes on pieces of paper, he would have written something different.

Geoffrey + Valerie = DANGER!

8 *School Dinners*

When Valerie came back from the Secretary's office, she was very quiet. She slipped into the seat Mrs Hemingway gave her – on the other side of the room from Marigold – and sat rigid and still, with her elbows tight against her sides. As soon as the bell rang for dinner, she put up her hand.

'I'm going home for dinner, Mrs Hemingway.'

'You are?' Mrs Hemingway frowned at her. 'Have you got a letter to say so?'

'I – oh!' Valerie went pink. Then she tried to look innocent. 'Do I need one?'

'Of course you do,' Mrs Hemingway said. 'It's perfectly clear in the school prospectus. Mrs Puddock's most particular about it. She never lets children out of school without a note.'

'I'll – I'll bring one tomorrow.'

Valerie's voice shook a bit. 'Can I go without one? Just for today.'

'Not just like that.' Mrs Hemingway frowned harder. 'We'd better go to the office and phone your mother. To check it's all right.'

Lee saw Valerie's eyes slide away sideways. Avoiding Mrs Hemingway's. 'We – we're not on the telephone.'

'Well, really!' Mrs Hemingway snorted. 'I suppose I'll have to take you round in my car then. To make sure there's somebody in when you get there.'

Valerie went very pale indeed. *Aha!* Lee thought. *You've trapped yourself.* When she was Mrs Puddock, she'd made sure that children couldn't get out of school without their parents knowing. Now she was caught by her own rules.

She couldn't take Mrs Hemingway to see her mother – because she didn't live with her mother. She was Mrs Puddock, and she lived on her own, with three cats and a budgie.

'I – ' She swallowed again. Lee could see her struggling to think of a way out of the awkward situation she'd got herself into. Suddenly, he felt really sorry for her.

'Can't she have a school dinner?' he said. 'And pay for it tomorrow?'

Mrs Hemingway beamed with relief. 'Oh, what a good idea! How about that, dear?'

'Yes,' Valerie said slowly. 'I – yes, that's fine.'

She still didn't look very happy, but it was her own fault. She'd made the rules, after all. Lee stopped worrying about her and concentrated on getting into the Hall for dinner. Without Mrs Puddock and Mr Merton to keep order, everyone was pushing to the front of the queue. If he let them get ahead of him, all the decent dinners would be gone.

He was just in time. He managed to grab a jacket potato and the last helping of sausages. After that it was all cheese pie and horrible, soggy school chips. Pulling a gloating face at Peanuts – who was just behind him, making sick noises at the cheese pie – he slid into a chair and started on the first sausage.

He was halfway through it when there was a loud noise from the dinner queue.

'I can't eat *that!* I'll have the most terrible indigestion!'

Valerie was standing with a plate of cheese pie and chips in her hand, trying to give it back to Mrs Longley, the cook behind the counter.

Mrs Longley just sniffed. She was a small, wiry grandmother, and she'd spent thirty years listening to children telling her why they couldn't eat school dinners.

'Get along with you!' She dipped her ladle into the cabbage pot and dumped a mound of soggy cabbage onto Valerie's plate. 'Children don't get indigestion.'

Valerie's eyes narrowed furiously. 'You don't know what you're talking about. Cheese flan gives me indigestion. Chips give me WORSE indigestion. And cabbage gives me WIND! I'm not going to eat any of it.'

'Please yourself.' Mrs Longley took the plate out of her hand and passed it on to the next person, who happened to be Geoffrey. 'I don't suppose you're so picky, are you, dear?'

Geoffrey looked down, rather queasily, at the mess of cheese and flan and cabbage and chips. 'I – '

'That's a good boy!' Mrs Longley patted his shoulder and pushed him away, towards Lee's table. 'Next!'

Valerie tapped sharply on the counter and picked up an empty plate. 'What about me? I haven't got anything to eat.'

Mrs Longley sniffed again. 'That's your choice, not mine. This isn't a hotel, you know. If you turn your nose up at what there is, you'll have to go hungry.' She reached across the counter and prodded Valerie in the stomach. 'You don't look as if you're going to fade away, any road up.'

Valerie's eyes looked as if they were going to pop out of her head. 'How DARE you speak to ME like that? I've never – '

But the rest of her sentence was lost because everyone in the Hall started laughing at Valerie as she stood there waving her plate and glaring at Mrs Longley.

And her fury had no effect at all. Mrs Longley simply whisked her ladle and flicked a piece of cabbage, as if by mistake, onto the back of Valerie's hand. 'I'll speak to you how I like. But you'd better watch how you speak to *me*, young lady, or you'll find your name in the Bad Book. Then you'll be sorry. Mrs Puddock can't abide rudeness.'

'She's already got her name in the Bad Book,' someone said helpfully.

Mrs Longley raised her eyebrows. 'Well, if she carries on like she's doing, she'll be the first person ever to get her name in twice.'

Valerie clenched a fist. 'I'm not scared of Mrs Puddock!'

'Aren't you, now?' Mrs Longley opened

her eyes very wide.

'Why should I be scared of her?' Valerie said defiantly. 'She's OK.'

Mrs Longley looked round, very slowly, at everyone else in the Hall. 'Did you hear that, children? We've got a tough one here. She's not afraid of Mrs Puddock. Have we got anyone else as brave as that? Hey? Hands up!'

No one moved. They all sat stock still, in case it was a trick question. And slowly, Valerie's shoulders drooped. She turned back to the dinner counter.

'You see?' Mrs Longley said, triumphantly. 'Now. Want some cheese pie after all?'

'No!' Valerie snapped. She grabbed an apple out of the fruit bowl and stomped across the Hall to sit down in the nearest chair, which happened to be next to Lee. Angrily and noisily, she bit into the apple, sitting with her eyes down and glowering at the table as she chewed.

Behind her, people were giggling and whispering and pointing, and some of them were doing imitations of her voice.

She didn't look round or say anything but Lee knew she'd heard because of the fixed set of her shoulders, and the slow, red flush that spread up the back of her neck. It seemed almost rude to be noticing that. Embarrassed, he looked away.

And he saw Marigold.

She was the very last person in the dinner queue and she was drifting along the counter looking as if she were going to burst into tears. Her hair was rumpled and she looked very small and waif-like.

'Please – ' She was too far away for Lee to hear her voice because she spoke so softly, but he saw her lips shape the word as she leaned across the counter towards Mrs Longley.

If it had been anyone else, Lee knew what would have happened. Mrs Longley was slightly deaf and she couldn't bear mutterers. She would have barked 'Speak up!' until the poor mutterer was forced to yell whatever it was.

But she didn't do that to Marigold.

She looked her up and down, briskly, and then leaned over the counter with her head tilted sideways so that Marigold could whisper into her good ear.

Fascinated, Lee posted a forkful of potato into his mouth and went on staring. He saw Mrs Longley lean back again and look Marigold up and down, with that sharp, steely gaze that made even Fred wriggle and shuffle his feet. But Marigold didn't wriggle or shuffle. She just went on staring at Mrs Longley with wide blue eyes.

And something extraordinary happened. Suddenly, Mrs Longley smiled. Then she turned and walked to the back of the kitchen where she always put her own plate of salad until the dinner hour was over. She came back with the plate in her hand and, with a nod, passed it across the counter to Marigold. Then, without a word, she picked up another plate and began to serve herself some cheese pie and cabbage and chips.

A small, self-satisfied, pussycat smile spread across Marigold's face. She came walking down the Hall towards Lee's table and sat down right next to Valerie.

No! Lee thought. *Don't sit there!* But he couldn't stop her. She sat down, put the plate of ham and salad on the table and picked up her knife and fork.

And Valerie saw what was on the plate.

Her hand stopped in mid-air, with the half-eaten apple just out of range of her mouth. In an icy voice she said, 'Where. Did. You. Get. That. Salad?' Every word separate, as though each one needed a separate enormous effort.

Marigold gave her an innocent, sugary smile. 'Mrs Longley gave me her own salad. Wasn't that nice of her? Because

I'm allergic to egg. And cheese.' She cut a small piece of ham off the thick, pink slice on her plate and smiled again.

'You're allergic – !' Valerie stopped, bright scarlet. Her next word was going to be a yell, Lee could see. Before she could get it out, he did the only thing he could think of.

'Here,' he said. 'Have this.' He jabbed a fork into his other sausage and held it out to her.

'What?' Valerie said. She blinked at him.

'The sausage,' Lee muttered. 'I can't eat two. I'm too full up.'

It was a ridiculous lie. He could have eaten six sausages with no trouble. And the moment the words were out of his mouth, he was sure that Valerie would yell at him. For being sorry for her.

But she didn't. She looked down at the sausage and then up at Lee's face. When she saw he wasn't laughing, she took the sausage.

'Thanks,' she said gruffly. Holding it on the fork, she began to eat it in small, careful bites.

She was still eating it when Lee finished his pudding. Geoffrey was struggling with the cheese pie as well, but Lee couldn't stay to see if he finished it because Mrs Longley spotted his empty plate.

'Come on now,' she called. 'Get outside if you've finished, Lee Godwin. You don't want to be stewing in here when you could be out in the fresh air.'

'That's *right*,' muttered Peanuts. 'Go outside and get some healthy frost-bite.'

Lee pulled a face at her and slid out of his chair. As he reached the door, he glanced back towards the table. Marigold was peacefully eating her way through her salad, but Geoffrey and Valerie both looked tired and miserable.

They can't stand this for long, Lee thought suddenly.

How long were they going to be eleven? Would they change back in a day or two, or would they have to grow up all over again, at the normal speed? And what happened at the end of school? Would they go home to empty houses, with no one to look after them?

Even if they worked out that the shoes had something to do with the change, they would still be stuck eating school cabbage. They'd still have to put up with getting told off if they behaved like adults. And suppose that went on for years . . .

Slowly, Lee walked down the corridor and pushed open the door to the playground.

And there was Joyce.

9 *Battle*

She was sitting on the pavement, outside the playground, with her back up against the school railings and all her tatty carrier bags arranged round her in a semi-circle.

For a second, Lee couldn't do anything except stare. He felt as though he'd imagined her, and he found himself shivering. Almost afraid to go any nearer.

Then, from the other side of the playground, he heard the unmistakable sound of her thin, scratchy cough, and the realisation hit him. It *was* her! She was the only person who really knew what was going on. He had to get her to explain!

He shot across the playground, desperate to reach her before she disappeared. As she heard his footsteps, she began to lever herself slowly off the ground, reaching for her bags, and he flung himself forward to snatch at the sleeve of her old coat. He grabbed it in time but he fell over, scraping his knees as he landed.

Joyce looked back at him, trying to drag her arm free. 'You again, is it? Wotcher falling around for this time?'

'You *know!*' Lee hissed. 'Tell me what's going on!'

'Going on?' Joyce narrowed her eyes, cunningly. 'Wotcher mean, going on?'

'With the teachers. And the shoes.'

Joyce grinned, baring her horrible teeth. 'Doncher think it's funny?'

'Of course I do,' Lee said. 'But – ' He stopped.

'Well?' Joyce looked sharply at him. 'Incher enjoying it? Getting yer own back?'

'Yes, but – '

'But what? Come on, spit it out.'

'Well – well, they're going to *guess*, aren't they? That I've got something to do with it.' Lee swallowed. 'They're not stupid, you know.'

'Not stupid? *Teachers?*' Joyce cackled. 'Do us a favour, boy. Most teachers haven't got a clue. And this lot's going to be too busy to guess anything. Much too busy.'

'They are?' Lee said doubtfully.

Joyce smacked at his hand. 'Trouble with you is yer always talking. Why doncher shut up and *watch?* Look over there.'

Lee turned round and saw Valerie walking briskly out of the school. A second later, the door flapped open again and Geoffrey marched through, hurrying to catch her up.

'There!' Lee said. 'What did I tell you? They're going to talk to each other. And once they do – '

'Watch!'

The door opened for a third time. It was Peanuts. For a second, she stood with a smile on her face, watching Geoffrey hurry after Valerie. Then, when he had almost caught up, she darted forward.

She was like lightning. Before Geoffrey had time to open his mouth, Peanuts had grabbed Valerie by the shoulders and spun her round.

'Here you are, Geoff!' she yelled. 'You like her, don't you? Why not get together?'

Even from the railings, Lee saw Geoffrey turn bright pink. He muttered something that was impossible to hear and began to back away.

Valerie was even pinker. She was struggling furiously and bellowing at full power. 'Get OFF! Let me GO, you silly little girl!'

Lee groaned. Now she was in for it. Peanuts would never stand for that.

He was right. Peanuts wasn't as large as Valerie but she was very, very strong. With a grin, she twisted Valerie's arm up behind her back. Then she pushed her forward, against Geoffrey's chest. 'Go on, Geoff,' she shouted, loud enough for everyone in the playground to hear. 'Give her a kiss!'

Valerie was outraged. 'Don't be RIDICULOUS!' With a gigantic effort, she wrenched her arm free, staggering backwards as she twisted away from Peanuts.

Unfortunately, that was exactly the moment that Fred chose to open the door for Marigold. Marigold came tripping through, looking over her shoulder to smile prettily at Fred, and Valerie cannoned straight into her. The two of them landed in a heap on the ground, with Valerie on top.

'*That's* more like it!' Joyce shrieked. She collapsed into hoarse laughter, slapping the ground with one hand. Then she peered at Lee. 'What's the matter, boy? Incher got a sense of humour?'

'Of course I've got a sense of humour!' Lee said indignantly.

'Why incher laughing then?'

'Because – because – '

Lee looked across the playground again. Fred had dragged Valerie to her feet. He was holding her by the scruff of the neck and yelling at her. And she looked – miserable.

'You're nothing but a bully!' Fred shouted. 'A great fat bully! Why d'you keep picking on Marigold?'

'It wasn't my fault!' Valerie yelled back. 'It was because of Pauline. She's the one you ought to be shouting at.'

Lee groaned again and buried his head in his hands.

'Toldjer,' Joyce said with satisfaction. '*She's* not going to have much time for guessing, is she? She's got her hands full just being eleven.' She leaned back, settling herself against the railings. Pulling a paper bag out of her cardigan pocket, she held it out to Lee. 'Want some popcorn?'

'This isn't the cinema!' Lee said crossly.

'Good as a film.' Joyce took a great handful of popcorn and crammed it into her mouth, chewing noisily.

Peanuts had started attacking Valerie too, just as Lee knew she would. She and Fred stood one on each side, bellowing at Valerie and prodding her in the ribs, and Valerie stood in the middle, yelling as loudly as both of them put together.

And then Geoffrey joined in.

He'd been standing on the edge of the group, looking uncomfortable and impatient as more and more people crowded round to watch. Suddenly, his hand shot out and he tapped Fred on the shoulder with one finger, waving him away from Valerie.

Lee couldn't hear what he said, but whatever it was it made the watching crowd roar with laughter, and Fred whirled round and gave him a hard shove.

To his amazement, Geoffrey shoved back. A second later, he and Fred were rolling over and over on the ground, scrapping as hard as they could.

'*That's* better,' Joyce muttered.

'Thought that Geoffrey was never going to start being normal.'

Lee stared at her. 'What d'you mean normal? He's going to get *hurt*. Anyone can see he's no good at fighting.'

Joyce sniffed. 'Better learn then, hadn't he? It's the other two you want to worry about. Them girls. That's where the real trouble's goingter be.'

The girls were certainly making more noise. Everyone in the playground must have been able to hear Valerie screeching at Peanuts.

'See what you've done! It's all your fault they're fighting. Troublemaker!'

Peanuts didn't yell back, but she gave a huge, beautiful grin that Lee understood perfectly. Valerie had been annoying her all day and now she was going to teach her a lesson. Clenching a fist, she lashed out, and the next moment she and Valerie were fighting as hard as the boys.

Lee began to scramble to his feet. 'We can't just sit here – '

'Keep yer hair on.' Joyce grabbed his arm and pulled him down again. 'They won't come to any harm. It's Madam who's the real little menace. Look at her over there in her ringside seat.'

She pointed across the playground. Marigold was sitting up with her arms round her knees, watching the fight with wide, innocent eyes. And a little, self-satisfied smirk on her face.

Lee struggled to pull his arm free. 'You don't understand. If Geoffrey and Valerie go on fighting, they're going to get into terrible trouble. And they haven't got a *clue* how to look after themselves. Someone's got to help them.'

Joyce tilted her head back and dropped the last handful of popcorn into her open mouth. 'Who's goingter help a couple of *teachers?*' she said scornfully. Crunching.

Lee took a deep breath, ready to argue with her, but there just wasn't time. Instead he jumped to his feet and began racing across the playground. He had to stop the fight – somehow – before any grown-ups came along. None of the teachers would put up with fighting, not even Mr Willoughby.

But Lee was only halfway there when the door swung open and there *was* Mr Willoughby in the doorway, looking harassed and irritable.

'Watch out, everyone!' Lee yelled, as loudly as he could.

That just made things worse. The crowd melted away immediately and the little group at the centre was left exposed to Mr Willoughby's eyes. Geoffrey fighting Fred. Valerie fighting Peanuts. And Marigold sitting there watching them.

Quick as a flash, while Mr Willoughby

was still taking in the scene, Marigold
jumped to her feet and ran towards him.

'Help!' she shrieked, in a shrill,
pathetic voice. 'They're all fighting. My
old school was never as rough as this!'

She flung herself at Mr Willoughby,
clutching desperately at his coat, and he
looked over at the four fighters.

'Get up!' he said. 'Get up *this instant!*'
And his voice was like thunder.

10 *Lee Speaks Out*

The four fighters struggled to their feet. They all looked terrible. Valerie's plaits were coming undone, Fred and Peanuts had buttons pulled off their shirts and Geoffrey had a big, dusty hole ripped in his navy-blue blazer. Mr Willoughby glared.

Fred and Peanuts didn't give him a chance to start telling them off. They both began their excuses, trying to shout each other down.

'It was Valerie's fault, Mr Willoughby, she started it – '

'Geoffrey just laid into me – '

'*Silence!*' Mr Willoughby roared. 'I don't want any excuses. You know we don't allow fighting here. It's Mrs Puddock's strictest rule. And as for fighting *new* children, on their first day – '

He was so horrified that, for a second, his voice failed. Fred and Peanuts started up again.

'But Valerie knocked Marigold over, and it's *her* first day too – '

'And Geoffrey was on Valerie's side – '

'*Someone* had to sort them out – '

'They're just a couple of bullies – '

Mr Willoughby hesitated. He looked at Valerie, taking in her big, square face and her beefy arms. Then his eyes flickered to Geoffrey, and Lee knew that he was remembering the beginning of the morning and how Geoffrey had tried to push his way into school.

And then he glanced down at Marigold who was still standing very close to him, looking small and frail. As if she needed protection.

He frowned. 'Well, Geoffrey? Well, Valerie? Is that what happened?'

'It wasn't quite like that,' Geoffrey said, in his crisp, precise voice. But before he could explain, Valerie opened her mouth.

No! Lee thought desperately. *No. Don't! Think before you speak!*

118

It was no use. Valerie snorted indignantly and glared at Marigold. 'Of course it wasn't like that! If Marigold hasn't got the sense to look where she's going – '

'You *see?*' Peanuts said smugly, turning to Mr Willoughby. 'Valerie thinks everyone ought to give way to *her*. She *needs* sorting out.'

Mr Willoughby looked uncertain. 'Has anyone got anything to add?' he said hopefully.

He couldn't see Fred and Peanuts glaring from behind him. *Just let anyone dare!* their expressions said. And all the watchers muttered and shuffled their feet and melted away to the other side of the playground.

Except Lee.

He found himself standing all alone, facing Mr Willoughby.

'Well, Lee?' Mr Willoughby said.

'I – ' Lee looked at Peanuts and Fred and they scowled even harder.

'He doesn't know a *thing*,' Peanuts said. 'Do you, Lee? He wasn't anywhere near.'

Fred nodded. 'He didn't come up until Valerie and Geoffrey had started fighting. *Did* you, Lee?'

Lee took a step backwards. It was going to be much easier to keep his mouth shut. To shake his head and pretend he hadn't seen anything.

And then he glanced sideways and saw Valerie's awkward, sulky face. And Geoffrey's stiff, pompous expression. They had no idea how to get a teacher on their side. They needed someone to help – and who would stick up for them if he didn't?

He swallowed. 'I *did* see. I was over by the railings and I saw it all. Peanuts was teasing Geoffrey and Valerie and then – it was an accident really. Honestly it was, Mr Willoughby. Valerie was just too close to the door when Marigold came through and – well, maybe Fred and Peanuts misunderstood.'

Mr Willoughby looked relieved. 'It sounds as if you all need to be more careful,' he said severely. 'I want everyone right away from these doors and playing foot – er – ' He coughed.

'I want everyone playing something sensible.'

He disappeared inside again. Peanuts glared at Lee, but all she said was, 'I'll get the football.' And she headed for the games cupboard.

Fred wasn't so easily distracted. He came marching up to Lee. 'What did you want to interfere for?' he growled. 'You didn't see a thing.'

'Yes I did,' Lee said stubbornly. 'I was only over there – ' He turned to point.

And immediately he forgot all about Fred. Because, over by the railings, Joyce was gathering up her bags. While he was wasting time arguing, she was getting ready to disappear again! Turning his back on Fred, Lee raced across the playground for the second time. He reached the edge just in time to grab Joyce's sleeve.

'You can't go yet! You haven't *told* me!'

Joyce scowled and wrenched at her arm. 'Get off! Wotcher mean I haven't toldjer? Haven't toldjer what?'

'You haven't told me what's going to

happen. To the teachers. How are they going to change back?'

Joyce rolled her eyes up at the sky. 'Kids! You want everything done for you. Thought you were fretting they might talk to each other. And guess it was you what sent them back to school.'

'Yes, I was, but – '

'Well, that's fixed, innit? What morjer want? Be asking me ter wipe yer nose for you next.'

'What d'you mean it's fixed?'

'Those three aren't goingter risk chatting to each other *now*. Take a look.'

Lee glanced over his shoulder. She was right. Valerie was edging away from Geoffrey and Marigold. Talking to them would mean teasing and trouble, and she obviously didn't want any more of that.

Geoffrey was looking warily at Marigold too. Lee could see he'd got the message that she was bad news.

'And Madam won't want anything ter do with them either,' Joyce said.

She stuck out her tongue in Marigold's direction and Lee looked that way.

Joyce was right. Marigold was ignoring the other two and keeping close to Fred, gazing up at him with admiring eyes. *Honestly*, Lee thought, *why can't he see through her? It's so obvious –*

And then Joyce bit his hand, hard, with her horrible teeth.

'Hey!' Automatically, Lee let go of her coat and whipped his hand back quickly through to his own side of the railings.

That was a mistake. He realised instantly, but it was too late by then. Joyce was on her feet and out of reach already, running down the road with her carrier bags bumping against her legs.

'Stop!' Lee yelled desperately. 'You can't just go off like that. You've got to tell me! *How can they change back?*'

Joyce glanced round, without stopping, with her teeth bared in a grin. 'Same way they got like that, of course!'

'What? What do you *mean?*'

Her voice was already faint. She was almost at the corner. But Lee just caught the words. '*Get the shoes . . .*'

Then she whipped round the corner

and vanished and he sat back on his
heels. He'd failed. All he knew was that
he had to get the shoes. Slowly he stood
up.

And, at that moment, Peanuts came
out of the school with a football tucked
under her arm. She looked straight
across the playground at Lee, glared at
him again and dropped the ball.

'Take that, you!' she yelled.

And she sent the ball speeding
towards him, with a huge kick. One of
her cannon-ball specials. Lee knew he
wasn't good enough to stop it. It was
much too fast. He braced himself,
waiting for it to slam into his legs.

But it never reached him.

Suddenly Geoffrey turned and raced towards it. Jumping into the air, he caught it on his chest, nudged it down onto one knee and juggled it onto the ground, keeping it under perfect control all the time.

Then he stood there, with his foot on the ball.

'What are you waiting for?' Lee yelled. 'Kick it!'

'I can't,' Geoffrey said. 'Football is – ' He stopped, but it was obvious what he meant.

'Don't be so daft!' Lee grinned. 'Why don't you enjoy yourself? Before your knees get too stiff! You're only young twice!'

Geoffrey gave him a sharp, startled look. Then, quite unexpectedly, a smile spread across his face. Not a tight little smirk, like Mr Merton's but an enormous, toothy grin. He began to dribble the ball straight across the playground.

Peanuts came at him, ready to tackle, but she didn't stand a chance. Geoffrey dodged around her, hooked the ball after him, casually, with his left foot, and headed for the goal that was chalked on the school wall.

But not *straight* for the goal. On the way, he dribbled the ball round everyone he met. It was like watching a demonstration. He swerved right and left, dodging first one person and then another and keeping the ball so close to his feet that it almost seemed glued to the toes of his shoes.

Lee's shoes.

Peanuts raced down the pitch and flung herself in front of the goal. Baring her teeth, she crouched with her arms stretched wide, making a personal thing out of it, as usual. No one was going to beat *her*.

And Geoffrey teased her.

He didn't grin, because he was concentrating totally on the ball, but he made her look utterly silly. He feinted right and left and then right again so that she had to dodge from one side to the other. Then, when she was completely off balance, he shot.

His timing was perfect. The ball shot past Peanuts' left ear and smacked against the wall with a rich, satisfying thud. And then Geoffrey did smile. He turned back to Lee with another enormous grin on his face.

Lee thought that he had never, in his whole life, seen anyone look so happy.

11 *Peanuts on the Warpath*

By the time they went back into school, Peanuts was in a filthy temper. Geoffrey had made her look a complete fool. She hadn't been able to get the ball away from him at all. And Fred had made things worse by grabbing Geoffrey to play on his team.

Peanuts and her side had lost 14–0.

She stormed into the cloakroom and kicked off her outdoor shoes. Lee watched as she pushed her feet into her trainers. The ones she'd taken off Marigold.

He had to have those trainers. And the shoes Geoffrey was wearing. And the shoes Valerie was wearing. But he hadn't got a clue how to get hold of them, and it wasn't going to be easy. Not with Peanuts in such a temper.

When they walked into the classroom,

Mrs Hemingway was looking very pleased with herself. She had a big rectangle of hardboard laid out across three of the tables. Beside it was the map of the local streets that they'd drawn last week, with Miss Cherry. Lee could see the fish and chip shop he'd done, with the wiggle in the front where Peanuts had nudged him while he was measuring the line.

'We're going to turn this map into a model,' Mrs Hemingway said brightly. 'Most of you can make the buildings, but first I need some people to copy the street plan onto the hardboard.'

She looked round the classroom, scanning heads and her eyes landed straight on Lee.

'You can do it,' she said. 'And how about Geoffrey? Let's see if you can be *sensible* sometimes, Geoffrey.' She said it so that it sounded like a joke, and some people laughed, but Lee knew that it wasn't really funny. She hadn't forgotten what Geoffrey had said to her.

Her eyes roamed over the class again. 'And you can help them, can't you,

Mary? And – let me see – yes, you can do it too, Pauline.'

'*Great!*' Peanuts said, with relish.

Lee's heart sank.

Peanuts came striding down the room to the hardboard, grinned triumphantly at Lee and Geoffrey, and took charge of everything. 'Right. One corner each. You go there, Mary. Lee can go opposite you and Geoff can be opposite me. OK? Let's get started.'

'Wait a moment.' Geoffrey frowned and held up his hand. 'Shouldn't we sort out the basic plan first? Do a bit of measuring?'

She picked up a pencil without waiting for anyone else and began to draw the first street in her corner.

'But – ' said Geoffrey.

Mary and Peanuts ignored him. Peanuts was drawing hard, and Mary started to sketch out the grid of streets by the park. Geoffrey watched them. He opened his mouth and Lee could almost hear the words that were waiting to come out. *You're making a mistake, Pauline. If you don't do things properly, they're bound to come out wrong. If you take my advice...*

Lee didn't dare to say anything because he knew that would make things worse. He held his breath.

Geoffrey hesitated for a moment, with a tight little frown in the middle of his forehead. Then he shrugged. Choosing a pencil, he began to draw too, carefully marking out his own corner so that he would finish in the centre of the board, with one side of the playground.

Maybe he *had* learnt something after all. Lee grinned and bent over the hardboard.

But Peanuts wasn't going to be satisfied with drawing quietly. She waited for ten minutes or so, while Mrs Hemingway organised the rest of the class into making buildings and models of people to stand in the streets. Then she snorted.

'Shove over, Geoff.'

Her long, vigorous pencil strokes had eaten up the whole of her quarter of the board and she was beginning to spill over onto Geoffrey's. She jabbed at him with her elbow and drew the end of the High Street over the line he'd put in to mark the edge of the playground.

Geoffrey raised one eyebrow at her. 'Look again, Pauline. *Is* that right? Hey? Where are you going to put the Arcade?'

That was pure Mr Merton. Even down to the dry little smile that usually made Peanuts look sheepish. But she didn't look sheepish this time. She scowled at Geoffrey and pushed him over, even further.

'I'm going to put it *here*, of course.' And she drew in the Arcade with heavy pencil strokes, right across three of his streets. Then she lifted her head defiantly. 'OK?'

Lee knew what she was up to. She wanted a fight. She was daring Geoffrey to argue with her.

In a tight little voice, Geoffrey said, 'I haven't got enough room to finish my streets now.'

'You'll have to draw them smaller then, won't you?' Peanuts said nastily.

Geoffrey took a deep breath. He glanced across the classroom at Mrs

Hemingway, and Lee could see him getting ready to make a fuss. There was going to be a big, enormous row, and Peanuts was going to get wild and shout, and Geoffrey was going to make her do the map properly, and Peanuts would never forgive him and . . .

But none of that happened. Geoffrey just shrugged again. 'Very well. If that's how you want it.'

Rubbing out half of his original pencil lines, he sketched in the school and the streets beyond, exactly the same as before, only smaller. They were half the size of the streets Peanuts had drawn, and they looked ridiculous.

'Great!' said Peanuts briskly. Lee could tell that she felt cheated but she wasn't going to let on. 'Now get some felt pens and we'll ink it in quickly so Mrs Hemingway can't make us fiddle around with it.'

Mary trotted off obediently and came back with four black felt pens. They all began to work again, inking in their own sections, and they'd almost finished when Mrs Hemingway came over to see how they were getting on. As soon as she caught sight of the map, she let out a great wail.

'Oh, you *silly* boy, Geoffrey! Why have you drawn your streets so small?'

'I – ' Geoffrey looked at Peanuts, but she didn't say anything. Her face was completely blank and innocent. Mrs Hemingway shook her head.

'You should have let me see it before you inked it in. Look, poor Pauline has had to make the High Street much too long, just to join up with your section.'

'But – ' Geoffrey began.

Then he stopped.

Mrs Hemingway flapped her hand crossly. 'Well, it's too late to do anything about it now. You finish off the streets, and I'll send some people across to start painting the grass and the roads.'

Geoffrey bent over his corner and Peanuts kicked him under the table.

'Stop smirking, you!' she said.

But he didn't react at all. Peanuts pulled a face at him and then looked round to see who was coming to do the painting. Her eyes lit up.

It was Valerie and Marigold.

As they came across, with half a dozen pots of paint, Peanuts squirmed into the place next to Valerie.

'I'll help you,' she said. She began to stir the pot of green paint, wiggling the brush juicily.

Valerie gave her a severe look. 'I don't want to see you doing anything stupid with that brush, Pauline.'

Lee almost groaned out loud. How could she say that sort of thing? She *knew* what Peanuts was like.

Peanuts went on grinning and squidging the brush up and down so that the paint splattered on the table. Valerie watched her warily. *Keep your mouth shut*, Lee thought desperately. *Don't say anything, and it might still be all right.*

It almost seemed as though Valerie had got the message. She lowered her head and began to paint very quietly, concentrating on filling in the space that was meant to be the park. Being very careful not to go over the edges.

135

Peanuts grinned and squidged a bit more, but she obviously didn't find it so interesting when Valerie wasn't watching. After a while, she let go of the brush and wiped her hands on her apron. Then she peered over at the river that Marigold was painting.

'You've done that wrong,' she said loudly. 'It's supposed to come right up to the banks. Where Valerie's painting the green. You've left a gap.'

Marigold went faintly pink. 'I know,' she said in a small voice. 'But – I didn't want to get in – in *anyone's way.*'

She looked sideways at Valerie who was taking up a lot of room as she bent over the park. And then she looked up at Peanuts and smiled her secret, sneaky smile. *We know what Valerie's like, don't we . . . ?*

The little monster! She was deliberately trying to cause trouble for Valerie, to get Peanuts on her side!

And Peanuts leapt on the chance she'd been given. She returned Marigold's smile and then grabbed Valerie's shoulder. 'Here, you! Give poor Marigold

a bit more room. Just because you're a ten-ton elephant, you don't have to crowd her.'

Valerie was caught completely off balance. She staggered sideways, clutching at the table to try and steady herself, and her hand hit the pot of green paint. It tottered, toppled over and rolled towards the edge of the table, with the paint beginning to spill out.

Lee grabbed at it. He ought to have been in time to stop it falling off the table. In fact, he *was* in time. But he suddenly saw a wonderful, glorious opportunity. Because Peanuts' feet were almost underneath the place where the paint pot was. If it fell just a little to the left, it would fall on top of them.

On top of her trainers.

Lee closed his fingers, without taking hold of the pot, and nudged it to the left. It sailed towards the floor, onto Peanuts's feet, and green paint poured out, all over her trainers. Peanuts gave a huge howl of rage. It was what she'd been waiting for. A reason to explode.

'WHAT DID YOU DO THAT FOR?'

Mrs Hemingway came waddling over and Peanuts waved her feet, squelching them down onto the floor. 'Look! Look what Lee's done!'

'Don't move!' Mrs Hemingway shrieked. 'Take them off at once and go and wash them!'

'Why should *I* go and wash them?' Peanuts said indignantly. Just as Lee had hoped she would. 'It's not *my* fault! Lee's the one who spilt the paint.'

'OK!' Lee pretended to be annoyed. 'I'll do them.'

He bent down and undid Peanuts' laces and she held her feet in a lordly way, letting him take the trainers off. Then he took them out into the cloak-room and washed them under the cold tap.

He'd done it. He'd got the first pair of shoes!

It was a pity they were the ones Marigold had been wearing. He wasn't sure that she *deserved* to change back into a grown-up. But the change might not work unless he had all three pairs of shoes. He didn't want to take any chances.

Walking down to the far end of the cloakroom, he slipped the trainers down behind the radiator. They were hidden there, but if he slid his hand down he could pull them out again when he'd got hold of the other two pairs.

12 *Toe-crunching*

By the time Lee got back to the classroom, the floor had been mopped up and most of the roads and the grass were painted. People were starting to hover round the hardboard, waving the models they'd made.

Fred had been making the school, of course. It was typical of him to pick the most important building. He was busy showing it off to everyone.

'I've stuck black wool round the edge of the roof. For the guttering. And I've drawn in the bushes on the walls. And put the right colour curtains at the windows of Mrs Puddock's office. And –'

'OK, bighead.' Peanuts pulled a face at him. 'We know you're wonderful.'

'I think it's lovely,' Marigold said. She reached out and stroked the edge of the model. 'You are clever. Don't take any notice of Peanuts.' She gave Fred a smile. *We know what Peanuts is like*.

Fred smiled back. *Yes, we know what she's like*. Peanuts pushed Marigold's hand away and prodded scornfully at Fred's model.

'It's too big.'

'No, it's not.' Fred leaned over the hardboard and dumped the school into the square that Geoffrey had marked out for the playground. The square that he'd had to make smaller, because Peanuts had stolen his space.

'You see?' he said. 'It fits.'

'No it doesn't.' Peanuts scowled. 'It takes up the whole playground. If that was a real school, the children would have to play in the road.

'So?' Fred said. 'That just means the playground's too small. And whose fault is that?'

Peanuts went bright red and shoved at him with her shoulder, pushing him sideways away from the hardboard. Automatically, Fred pushed back, stamping on her foot.

Maybe he'd remembered that she

didn't have any shoes on. Maybe he hadn't. Either way, it didn't make any difference. *Crunch* went his foot, hard down onto her toes. Peanuts yelled at the top of her voice. She couldn't stamp back in her socks, so she picked up a chair instead and jabbed it at Fred's ankle.

'You little – !' Fred kicked out again, and Peanuts shrieked.

'Mrs Hemingway! He's stamping on me! Make him take his shoes off!'

Until then, Lee had been keeping well clear of them, but suddenly he saw another chance. Maybe they *all* ought to take their shoes off!

Lee moved like lightning. With his right foot, he stamped on Fred's toe as hard as he could. At the same time, with his left arm, he shoved Valerie sideways, catching her completely off balance. She staggered forward and one of her heavy, clumsy feet crashed down onto Marigold's thin black pumps. The other – oh hooray! – landed hard on Peanuts' toes.

'Mrs Hemingway!' Peanuts yelled.

'They're all doing it. Everyone's stamping on my feet.'

Lee gave one last shove. This time it was Mary he pushed. She tottered, put a foot back to steady herself and landed up treading on his foot.

'Ouch!' he said, as loudly as he could. Then he stood back and waited to see what would happen.

Mrs Hemingway lumbered across the classroom, glowering at them. She was beginning to look frayed and tired. 'What's the matter *now*? Did you say someone had been stamping on people's feet, Pauline? Who's been stamping on who?'

'Whom,' Geoffrey said, under his breath.

143

Mrs Hemingway whisked round and blinked at him. 'What?'

'Who's been stamping on *whom*,' Geoffrey said again. Politely. 'You have to use the accusative, you know. For the one who's stamped on.'

That was too much for Mrs Hemingway's temper. 'You silly little boy!' she snapped. 'Go and sit in the book corner on your own. *Without* reading.'

Geoffrey shrugged and walked away, and Mrs Hemingway turned back to the others. 'Now then. Who's been stamping on *who*?'

There was an uproar.

Fred pointed at Lee.

Lee pointed at Mary.

Marigold pointed at Valerie.

Peanuts pointed at Fred and Valerie.

There were fingers pointing every-where. Mrs Hemingway sighed loudly and rolled her eyes up at the ceiling.

'What a lot of *babies* you are. I think all of you had better take your shoes off.'

Valerie looked outraged. 'But that's

not fair. *I* didn't stamp on anyone's toes.'

'You stamped on mine!'

Peanuts and Marigold said it together. Peanuts with loud, juicy relish and Marigold in a grieved, pathetic little voice.

'But that wasn't my fault!' Valerie looked even more outraged. 'Lee pushed me!'

Mrs Hemingway frowned. 'Well, Lee?'

Lee looked down at Valerie's gleaming, polished toecaps. He didn't usually tell lies, but he'd made up his mind he was going to get those shoes. And he couldn't think of any other way.

'I didn't push her!' he said, managing to sound even more injured than she did. 'She pushed *me*, if you really want to know.'

For a second, Valerie was completely speechless. Her mouth opened and shut, but no sound came out. She looked as if she couldn't believe what he'd said.

Which was peculiar, really. When she was Mrs Puddock she heard children

145

having arguments like that every day.

Mrs Hemingway didn't give her a chance to get her voice back. 'Come on! Shoes off, all of you. Otherwise *I'll* stamp on your toes.'

That was quite a threat, because her large, heavy body was supported on two spiky little heels. *Ouch*! thought Lee. He slipped off his shoes as quickly as he could.

And then he realised what was wrong with his idea.

Valerie was unlacing her shoes and taking them off, just as he'd planned. But that didn't mean he could get them away from her. She lined them up on the floor, side by side, right next to where she was standing. There was no chance of sneaking them away from there.

He'd have to do something else. And that would mean more trouble. Oh well.

Leaning towards Fred, he hissed, 'Bet I can throw my shoes right over to the book corner. Bet I can get them further than you can.'

Fred could never resist a challenge like that. 'Bet you can't!' In one smooth movement, he sent his left shoe skimming across the classroom.

Before Mrs Hemingway could say anything, Lee lobbed one of his shoes over to the bookcase and sent the other spinning under the Nature Table. Then

he turned to Mrs Hemingway with his eyes wide open, innocently.

'Just tidying them away.'

It was lucky teachers were so predictable. Anybody normal would have wondered why he'd done something like that, especially when he'd just been told off. He could see Peanuts and Mary staring at him, amazed. But Mrs Hemingway came out with just the answer he'd wanted, as if he'd pressed a button.

'I don't think we want that kind of tidying up. Do we? You can all go and put your shoes neatly in the cloakroom. And if there's any more trouble, you'll *all* get your names in the Bad Book.'

Lee had to struggle to stop himself grinning. Done it! He could easily get Valerie's shoes now, as long as he was last out of the classroom. And that would be simple because he had to collect his shoes. If he made enough fuss about that, everyone else would be out of the way by the time he got to the cloakroom.

He pretended that it was very difficult to get the shoe that was under the Nature Table, wriggling about on the carpet and straining to reach it. In the end, he managed to look so clumsy that Mrs Hemingway came across to hold the table, in case he tipped it up. By the time he stood up, with the shoe in his hand, everyone else was already coming back from the cloakrom.

'Oh, do hurry up!' Mrs Hemingway said. 'Or there won't be time for a story.'

He did more than hurry. He sprinted like an Olympic athlete, dived into the cloakroom, threw his shoes under his peg and looked round frantically for Valerie's.

There they were. Lined up neatly, side by side. He grabbed them, chucked them behind the radiator, with Peanuts' trainers, and then sauntered back to the classroom, trying not to look out of breath. Two pairs down and one to go. All he had to do now was get Geoffrey's shoes.

But there wasn't much time left. After the story, they would all be going home. He had to think of something fast.

When he walked back into the classroom, the others were already sitting on the carpet in the book corner. Geoffrey was at the back, with his legs together and his arms round his knees. Lee looked at the two battered shoes on his feet. How was he going to get them off?

He didn't realise how hard he was staring until Geoffrey glanced up suddenly. And saw where he was looking.

Geoffrey didn't say anything, but he looked thoughtful. And very suspicious. Moving round sideways, he tucked his feet underneath him.

13 *Last Chance*

Lee sat down beside Geoffrey and Mrs
Hemingway looked up.

'Be quick now. We should just have
time for a whole chapter, if you all behave.'

'Oh, *good*,' Fred muttered sarcastically, under his breath.

Peanuts pulled a face. They all knew
what to expect. Mrs Hemingway was a
terrible reader, and even *Redwall* would
sound boring once she got going on it.
She read everything in the same dull,
flat voice, and she skipped over bits that
she thought were unimportant.

Briskly, she opened the book. After the
first half-page, people began to fidget
and mutter. After two pages, even
Geoffrey was looking bored. He pulled a
piece of paper out of his pocket and
began to scribble something on it with a
pencil stub.

Lee was the only person who wasn't wriggling. He sat very still because he was thinking. He kept staring down at those scuffed shoes. How was he going to get hold of them? How was he going to make Geoffrey take them off?

He'd only got a few minutes left to think of a plan.

He stared sideways, watching Geoffrey's pencil moving across the paper. And suddenly he decided to stop being careful. He had to take a chance or it would be too late. He waited for the next time Geoffrey glanced up from the paper – pretending to be listening to the story – and then his hand shot out.

He grabbed the paper, turned it over without looking at what was written on the front, and scribbled a quick message. *Want to see some magic? If you give me your shoes, I can turn you into a grown-up*. Then he pushed it back.

Geoffrey looked down at the paper and went very, very still. Almost as if he'd stopped breathing. His eyes flickered as he read the message again. And again.

Nervously, Lee watched the bent head, with its clumsy, old-fashioned haircut, waiting for Geoffrey to look up. Waiting to meet those questioning, suspicious eyes.

But Geoffrey didn't look up. Instead he scribbled something on the paper and handed it back to Lee.

Who says I want to be a grown-up?

Lee frowned. 'Everyone wants to be grown-up,' he whispered softly.

But he didn't whisper softly enough. Mrs Hemingway might be a dull reader, but there was nothing dull about her ears. Her head jerked up.

'Lee? Was that you?'

'No, I – ' Lee began.

And then he had a wonderful inspiration. Geoffrey wasn't going to give him the shoes – *but he could get them anyway*. It was so obvious that he couldn't believe he hadn't thought of it before. It was a real effort not to smile, but he managed it, forcing his face into a scowl.

'Yes, I was talking,' he said, in an injured voice. 'I was telling Geoffrey to give me my shoes back.'

Mrs Hemingway sighed impatiently. 'How can Geoffrey have your shoes? You've taken them out to the cloakroom.'

'Not my indoor shoes,' Lee said. 'My outdoor shoes.' He scowled harder. 'Geoffrey's wearing them. Look.'

Geoffrey frowned and tucked his feet even further underneath his body. It was all Lee could do not to grin.

'They are mine!' he said. 'Make him take them off and I can prove it.' He turned triumphantly to Geoffrey. 'I can prove it – because they've got my name in!'

Geoffrey's mouth twitched. For a second, Lee thought he was going to smile, but he didn't. Instead, reluctantly, he uncoiled his legs and began to unknot the old, frayed laces. It wasn't very easy. Lee had never bothered to undo his shoes, and those knots had been there for months.

Finally, the left-hand lace came undone, and the right-hand one snapped. Slowly, Geoffrey slipped the shoes off and looked inside.

'There isn't a name,' he said quickly.

'Yes there is!' gabbled Lee. 'It's underneath the tongue. That's where my mum always writes it. Let me show you –'

Mrs Hemingway reached over and took the shoes before he could touch them. Lee held his breath. He knew they were his shoes, but things were so peculiar today that he couldn't be quite sure . . .

'*Lee Godwin*,' Mrs Hemingway read out, in a loud voice.

'You see?' Lee said, looking round at Geoffrey. He couldn't resist grinning. 'Naming things saves *such* a lot of trouble. Doesn't it?' And he reached out his hand for the shoes.

But Mrs Hemingway didn't pass them over. 'I don't think you need them just now,' she said primly. 'We've had enough trouble with shoes for one day. I'll keep them here safely for the time being. You can stay behind at home-time and we'll sort the whole thing out then.'

She bent down and slipped the shoes underneath her chair.

That was no use! Lee's heart sank. If he had to stay behind, Valerie and Peanuts would get to the cloakroom ahead of him. They'd be crashing round, hunting for their shoes, and he wouldn't stand a chance of smuggling them out. What could he do? If he messed this up, he'd never get hold of all three pairs again.

And he'd only got five minutes to work something out.

For a moment, he was tempted to give up. After all, what did it matter to him? Geoffrey and Marigold and Valerie could stay eleven for ever, for all he cared. Why was he going to all this trouble to help them change back?

Then he saw Peanuts grinning. Very gently, she was untying the ribbons on the ends of Valerie's plaits. As he watched, she lifted one corner of the cloth on the Nature table and began to knot the ribbons round it. When Valerie stood up, there was going to be an appalling crash, with water and mud flying everywhere. Peanuts might get into trouble, but she wouldn't care. She'd have made Valerie look a fool. Again.

And Geoffrey . . .

Geoffrey was all right. He'd gone back

to scribbling on his piece of paper. But Fred was watching him carefully. Suddenly he leaned sideways and whispered, very softly, into Lee's ear.

'Geoff's writing a poem. Reckon it's about Valerie?' And he grinned. A grin that meant more trouble for Geoffrey and Valerie at home-time.

It's no use, Lee thought hopelessly. Geoffrey and Valerie would never survive if they stayed like that. They might be tough and horrible grown-ups, but they weren't tough enough to be eleven. They couldn't stand the teasing. And they'd got no idea how to tease back. Marigold was the only one of them who could cope.

And he wasn't sure he wanted sly,

sneaky Marigold in his class for ever.

He sat very still, listening to Mrs Hemingway's voice droning on and on, and he stared at the shoes tucked away under her chair. There was only one way to get them in time. It was risky, but he was sure he could do it if he was quick enough. As long as he picked the right moment.

He waited until Mrs Hemingway got near the bottom of a page so that she was concentrating hard, with her hand hovering, ready to turn over. Then he launched himself forward at her chair. Pushing her fat legs out of the way, he grabbed the shoes and jumped up. Then he ran out of the classroom as fast as he could.

He was through the door before anyone else made a move. What he had done was so terrible that for a moment everybody was stunned. He heard Mrs Hemingway squeal as he reached the door, but he didn't look round to see what she was doing. He just launched himself down the corridor towards the cloakroom to get the other pairs of shoes.

What on earth had made him hide them in such an awkward place? His heart thudded as he scrambled to the radiator and felt down behind it. Suppose they'd gone? Suppose they'd slipped down so far that he couldn't reach? Suppose . . . ?

It was all right. They were still there. But as he scooped them out he realised he couldn't carry all three pairs without a bag. Leaping to his peg, he unhooked his empty shoe-bag.

And that was when Geoffrey appeared.

There were no footsteps to hear because Geoffrey wasn't wearing shoes. Suddenly, without any warning, Lee looked round and there he was, at the entrance to the cloakroom, staring straight at him.

At his armful of shoes.

Lee had a mad, hysterical desire to laugh. He could just imagine what he looked like. A crazy shoe-o-holic. Maybe he should grab lots of other pairs, to confuse Geoffrey even more.

As he pushed his feet into the indoor shoes under his peg, he dropped Peanuts' trainers on the floor.

He snatched them up but Geoffrey's eyes widened.

'That's what Marigold was wearing,' he said slowly. 'You've got Marigold's shoes, and Valerie's and –'

'I'm trying to help,' Lee said. 'You ought to be grateful.'

'*Grateful?*' With a strange noise that was half a gasp and half a squeal, Geoffrey launched himself forward, grabbing at the shoes. Lee reacted automatically, without thinking. Pushing the shoes into his shoe-bag, he charged forward to meet Geoffrey, because that was the only way out.

And when they met, he pushed, as hard as he could. He didn't really expect to make much of an impression, and his fists were already starting to bunch for the fight that would come next. But Geoffrey wasn't wearing any shoes. His feet skidded on the hard floor of the cloakroom and he staggered sideways, falling against the pegs.

That was all Lee needed. He had no real idea of what he was going to do next.

All he knew was that he had to get out of the school as fast as he could. He could already hear a noise from the classroom and when he swung out of the cloakroom he saw a gaggle of people heading down towards him. Mrs Hemingway. Peanuts. Valerie and Marigold.

Out!

There was no point in saying anything. Putting his head down, he turned and ran, tearing across the playground and out of the gate, with the shoe-bag banging against his legs. Pushing his way through the mothers waiting at the gate, he headed down the High Street.

Towards the Arcade.

14 *Snatch and Grab*

The street was full of parents with pushchairs heading for the school. Lee dodged and weaved between them, trying to stay out of range of anyone who might try to catch him. He was pretty sure he was all right now that he'd left the playground. He didn't think Mrs Hemingway would come wobbling down the road after him, and he couldn't see her letting the children out either. Not before home-time. Geoffrey was the only person who might have followed, but he hadn't got any shoes.

It ought to be safe to stop running.

Slowing down, Lee glanced over his shoulder – and realised how wrong he was. Even without his shoes, Geoffrey hadn't given in. He was charging up behind, pounding the pavement with his socked feet.

Lee bounded off again, but it was too late. It took him a couple of seconds to get up to speed and, by that time, Geoffrey was only a few metres behind. And he was a faster runner. Just before the Arcade, he caught up, and his hand reached out to snatch the bag.

Lee held on grimly, but that didn't make any difference. With one desperate tug, Geoffrey pulled the shoe-bag away from him, snapping the worn, frayed string. Then before Lee could grab back, he ran on ahead.

Lee followed automatically, not really expecting to catch up. He'd seen Geoffrey run flat out before, when they were playing football, and he knew that there was no way he was going to catch him. But he felt that he had to keep the shoe-bag in sight for as long as he could.

By the time Geoffrey swung round the corner into the Arcade, Lee was a good fifty metres behind and horribly out of breath. He was about to give up and go home.

But then he heard the thump.

A thump. Then a gasp from Geoffrey.

163

And then a familiar, moaning voice.

'Doncher *never* watch out? You boys – you're all the same.'

Lee sprinted to the corner and stuck his head round.

Joyce was sitting in the same place where he'd first seen her, with her back up against the wall and her hands clamped firmly over Lee's red and white striped shoe-bag. And next to her, dragging himself off the ground and rubbing his elbow, was Geoffrey.

Geoffrey didn't see Lee because he had his back to the High Street. But Joyce did. Her surprising, bright eyes glittered up at Lee, but she didn't say a word to show he was there. It was Geoffrey she spoke to, and her voice was as sharp as ever.

'Well? Incher going ter say yer sorry?'

Geoffrey had obviously hurt his elbow quite badly and he snapped back at her. 'If you *will* sit in such a stupid place – !'

Joyce tossed her head. 'Well, pardon me for living. I don't suppose *you* ever got tripped over because you were in a stupid place.'

'I wouldn't hang around anywhere so daft – ' Geoffrey began. Then, quite suddenly, he stopped.

'Hah!' Joyce said. She leaned forward and hissed at him. 'Never hung around outside a door? Never had yer feet tripped over?'

Lee could tell, even from the back of his head, that Geoffrey was remembering what had happened yesterday. When Lee had tripped over his feet. He *had* been standing in a stupid place, too close to the door.

Joyce's hands closed even more tightly round the bag and she sniffed. 'Oughter make you go back and come round that corner again, didn't I? Slowly.'

This time, when Geoffrey answered, his voice was quite different. 'I'm sorry I fell over you,' he said politely. 'May I have my bag back now?'

'*That's* better,' Joyce said with satisfaction. She pulled the top of the bag open and tipped the shoes out. '*Three* pairs of shoes!' she said. As if she didn't know anything about them. As if she had never seen the bag and the shoes before.

'Please – ' Geoffrey held out his hand, but she ignored it and peered at his feet instead.

'Pretty funny thing to do. Running around in socks when yer carrying three pairs of shoes. Incher got no sense?'

Geoffrey turned, trying to grab the bag – and saw Lee standing at the entrance to the Arcade. For a moment, they stared at each other.

'No,' Geoffrey said softly. 'I haven't got quite as much sense as I thought I had. But I think I'm getting better. Don't you, Lee?'

'I think – ' Lee swallowed. Suddenly, what he said seemed very important. He wanted to get it right. When he spoke again, his voice was gruff. 'You're OK. Pretty weird for an eleven-year-old, but – OK.'

For a split second, Geoffrey smiled. Not his tight, Mr Merton smile, but that wonderful, happy, football smile. Then Joyce sniffed again.

'You'll do,' she said. 'Gissa hand up

now. Then you can have yer bag back.'

Geoffrey turned away from Lee again and bent down, stretching out an arm to help her. Over his shoulder, Joyce glanced up at Lee – and he *knew*.

This was it. They were back at the beginning. This was just what had happened yesterday, when she took the shoes. If he let it go on, the same things would happen, all over again. And Geoffrey and Valerie and Marigold would change back into grown-ups.

That was what he wanted. Wasn't it?

Lee stood there, like someone watching a play. Joyce held up her grubby hand and Geoffrey hauled on it, dragging her to her feet and scattering her carrier bags all over the ground. They tumbled over, of course, and showers of rubbish cascaded across the coloured paving slabs. Bundles of rags and stockings. And lots of crumpled newspaper.

'There!' Joyce said crossly, pulling her hand free. 'Now you'll run off, woncher, and I'll have ter pick up all that stuff meself.'

She bent over and began to scrabble at the mess, and Geoffrey – of course – bent over to help, turning away from her as he scooped up her horrible rubbish. Joyce still had the shoe-bag in her hand and she pulled the top wide open. Then she looked up at Lee again.

His whole head filled with pictures.

Mr Merton's cold face, with its thin, tight-lipped smile. *Write me a poem by tomorrow morning. With at least twelve lines. And rhymes* . . . that slow walk, as he climbed the steps on his creaky knees . . .

Geoffrey's fierce attack on Mrs Hemingway. *I can't* bear *teachers who waste children's time* . . . the wonderful way he dribbled the football . . . his huge, happy smile . . .

No! Lee felt as if his head was going to burst open. Geoffrey didn't have to go back to being Mr Merton! He could be warned. It would only take one shout to make him spin round and grab the shoe-bag, and then he would be safe. Safe in his shorts, with his legs that could run and his face that could smile. If he kept those battered lace-ups, he

could stay young. And –

And what?

Very slowly, giving Lee plenty of time to speak, Joyce bent down and picked up a handful of crumpled newspaper. Geoffrey's back was still turned as she pushed the paper into the shoe-bag and pulled the string tight at the top. Then she picked up the shoes.

Watch out, Geoffrey! She's stealing the shoes!

But the words wouldn't come. Lee stood there, dumb, as Joyce tossed the shoes into one of her carrier bags. Then Geoffrey turned round and she began to shuffle away out of the Arcade, leaving the two boys staring after her.

As she turned the corner, Geoffrey's hand reached for the shoe-bag.

'It's not – ' Lee began. Then he stopped. He saw Geoffrey's face change as he lifted the bag and felt how light it was. 'Sorry,' he said.

For a moment, Geoffrey was quite still, staring down at the striped bag in his hand. He didn't bother to open it. His mouth curved into a thin, rueful smile.

'Oh well,' he said. 'You can't be eleven for ever. Here.' He tossed the shoe-bag to Lee. Then he hesitated.

'I'm sorry,' Lee said again. 'I – ' He hunted for some better words. 'It was good playing football with you.'

Geoffrey shrugged and put a hand into his pocket. 'I didn't think you were going to need this, but you will now. Use it for – well, you'll see what for.' He pulled out a piece of paper and passed it to Lee.

'That?' Lee looked down at it, puzzled. It was the paper he'd written the message on.

Want to see some magic? If you give me your shoes, I can turn you into a grown-up.

170

Who says I want to be a grown-up?

Geoffrey didn't explain. He just pushed the paper into Lee's hand. Then he turned and walked away up the Arcade. Halfway along, there was an old, crumpled Coke can lying against the wall. With one toe, he scooped it up. Even though he hadn't got any shoes, he began to dribble it ahead of him, down the Arcade.

Lee stood and watched him. Watched the quick, neat movements of his feet and his skinny bare legs as he swung out into Birmingham Street at top speed, with the Coke can under tight control. As if it were glued to the toes of his socks.

When he had completely gone and the sound of the clattering can died away, Lee unfolded the piece of paper and turned it over to look at the other side.

Fred had been right. It was a poem. But it wasn't about Valerie. It was a poem exactly twelve lines long, with rhymes, and it was headed: *Feet*

Lee stood and read it.

When you are young, they bounce along
Where you want to go.
Boot your ball and jump the wall,
Run and kick and grow.

Later on, the road seems long
And your feet are not so new.
They may grow sore, but you've got no
    more –
They have to take you through.

When you are old, your toes get cold
And arthritis strikes, and gout.
It's easy to lose your dancing shoes
When your feet can't skip about.

He stared down at it for a long time, remembering the sound of the Coke can clattering up the Arcade. It was a better poem than he could ever have written. But somehow it wasn't – quite right. It didn't sound finished.

Very slowly, he walked down the Arcade, juggling words in his mind as he headed home.

15 *Feet*

Lee pulled on his coat and picked up his bag. 'Bye, Mum!' he called. 'I'm going now.'

His mother stuck her head round the kitchen door. 'But you're *early*!' She looked at him as if he might be ill.

'Got some things to do. Got to give that poem to Mr Merton.'

'I thought you did that yesterday.'

'He – ' Lee hesitated. 'He wasn't around yesterday. But he'll be there today. I'm sure. See you after school.'

He ducked out before she could say anything, and marched off up the road. Because he was so early, he didn't see anyone he knew. Birmingham Street was deserted and the Arcade was completely empty, but somehow that didn't surprise him. He had a feeling that he wasn't ever going to see Joyce sitting on the paving slabs again.

It was only when he turned out into the High Street that he saw a familiar figure ahead of him at the school gate. Not Joyce, but a huge bulky figure, like a tank wearing a flowery dress. It was Mrs Puddock, looking just the same as she always had until yesterday.

Except that she wasn't quite the same. She was standing in the gateway, glancing down uncertainly at her clothes.

Mrs Puddock was *hesitating*! She was checking that she really was her proper, grown-up self.

Lee had a very strange feeling, as if he were seeing two people. Not just Valerie Puddock – the terrifying tank in the flowery dress – but poor, lumpy, awkward Valerie Pilkington too. The girl she'd been before she grew up and got married and turned into a teacher. *It's all right*, he wanted to say. *It's all over. You're safe now.* But he couldn't say that. She'd be horrified if she guessed that anyone knew about yesterday.

He knew what he could say, though. Beaming all over his face, he marched up to the gate.

'Good morning, Mrs Puddock.'

He expected her to look relieved, but he wasn't prepared for her enormous smile. She beamed at him.

'What a nice way to be greeted first thing in the morning. You deserve something special, for being so cheerful.' She opened her big shopping bag and, with a flourish, she pulled out a notebook. A medium-sized blue notebook. 'I'm going to write your name in here.'

Lee's mouth fell open. He couldn't believe it. She was going to write his name in the Bad Book!

Then she opened the notebook and he saw that it wasn't the Bad Book at all. It was the same kind of blue notebook, but there were gold stars stuck all over the cover. Smiling at him, Mrs Puddock began to read out the message inside.

'This is the GOLD Book. You are having your name written in it because you have done something ESPECIALLY

good. CONGRATULATIONS!'

Lee swallowed. 'The, the Gold Book?'

'That's right.' Mrs Puddock beamed again and wrote his name in it, in large, bold letters. 'It's no good just telling people off. They need ENCOURAGING. So I'm going to throw away the Bad Book and have this instead. Do you think – ' Just for a second, she hesitated again. ' – do you think it's a good idea?'

Lee grinned at her. 'It's a brilliant idea!'

'Thank you, Lee.' Mrs Puddock straightened her shoulders and snapped the book shut. Then she looked up at the school. 'Ah! There's Mr Willoughby!'

Mr Willoughby had just opened the front door. He peered out nervously and when he saw Mrs Puddock at the gate he turned pale and ducked back inside.

'Poor man!' Mrs Puddock said briskly. 'He must have had a DREADFUL time yesterday, with three of us away. I'd better go and thank him.'

She sailed across the playground, still smiling, and Lee stared after her. Amazed. Why was she being so nice?

Could it have anything to do with the way he'd spoken to her? He hadn't said anything special. And yet – he wouldn't have said anything at all before. He'd just have skulked past, expecting her to be angry, while she got crosser and crosser.

Like Valerie.

Thoughtfully, Lee walked into the playground. Fred was there already, staring down at a thick, heavy chalk line drawn across the middle of the playground.

'What's that for?' Lee said.

Fred shrugged. 'Search me. It was like that when I got here.' He tapped it with one foot. 'Bet you can't hop all the way along it without falling off.'

'Bet I can!'

Lee ran to the end of the line and began to hop, holding his arms out at the sides to balance himself. But he was only half the way along when a voice called out from the doorway.

'Lee! Are you *very* busy? Or can you give me a hand?'

It was Miss Cherry, standing at the

top of the steps with a huge pile of books in her arms. They looked as if they were going to tumble to the ground at any moment. Lee darted forward to rescue them. *Poor Miss Cherry*, he thought —

And then, suddenly, he had that double vision again. She was Miss Cherry all right, but she was Marigold too. Standing with her head tilted sideways and her shoulders drooping, to make him feel sorry for her. Fixing him with her big blue eyes so that he would do what she wanted.

Miss Cherry could manage those books perfectly well, but she was going to dump them on him. If he let her.

Lee pushed his hands into his pockets, out of the way, and walked the rest of the way up the steps. When he got to the top, he said, 'Give me half of those. I can't manage any more than that, but I'll carry half for you.'

'Oh, goodness me!' Miss Cherry's silvery laugh trilled down at him. 'You're underestimating yourself, I'm sure. A big strong boy like you can easily manage them all.'

'Not if a big strong woman like you can't,' Lee said, politely. 'Your arms are longer than mine.'

'Really?' Miss Cherry laughed again. 'Let's see. Hold them out.'

Lee took his hands out of his pockets. 'Half,' he said firmly. And stretched his arms out.

Miss Cherry looked at him. Then, very carefully, she slid half the books into his arms. Together, the two of them began to walk along the corridor, towards the classroom.

'Things are in a bit of a muddle,' Miss Cherry said. 'You had Mrs Hemingway

yesterday, didn't you? And I hear Mr Willoughby was in charge.' She gave Lee her quick, secret smile.

Lee nearly grinned back. It would have been so easy to do. *Yes. they're useless, aren't they?* But he remembered Marigold and her sly, sneaky smiles.

'Mrs Hemingway's OK,' he said stoutly. 'It must be quite difficult being called in like that, without any warning. And Mr Willoughby managed really well.'

Miss Cherry blinked, as if he'd surprised her. *Good!* Lee thought. Walking into the classroom, he dumped the books on her desk and turned round quickly.

'I'm sorry but I can't help you tidy the classroom. I have to look for my outdoor shoes. They got lost yesterday.'

'But you ran off with them,' Miss Cherry said. 'You – '

Then she remembered that she wasn't supposed to have been there yesterday. She stopped and turned bright pink.

Lee grinned at her, enjoying himself. 'Oh, there was a lot of trouble about shoes yesterday. There was even a silly little girl called Marigold who turned up in Peanuts' precious trainers.'

'Goodness,' Miss Cherry said faintly. 'I hope she won't do it again today.'

'Oh, she won't,' Lee said. 'We won't be seeing any more of her.' With another grin, he walked through the door and down towards the cloakroom.

It didn't take him long to find his shoes. They were where he knew they'd be. Lined up neatly underneath his peg. Just as Fred's were underneath his peg, and Peanuts' trainers were underneath hers.

He pulled them out and looked at them. The toes were even more scuffed than they'd been last time he wore them. As though someone had been playing football in them, very hard. And the right lace was knotted and snapped off short. He put his finger under the short, frayed end and flipped at it.

'Time you had some new laces,' said a dry voice behind him.

He turned round and saw Mr Merton staring down at him – and he didn't know what to say.

Because Mr Merton looked exactly the same as he'd always looked. There was no double vision there. Lee looked up into his eyes and couldn't see any remnant of Geoffrey at all. Suddenly, everything that had happened yesterday seemed impossible.

Mr Merton gazed down at him gravely for a moment. Then he smiled. Not Geoffrey's big grin, but not his usual, cold, tight smile either. He looked cautious and uncertain.

'What about the poem you were writing for me? Have you got that?' he said.

Lee hesitated. 'Ye–es. I didn't write it all myself, but – '

He didn't know what else to say, so he reached into his pocket and pulled out the paper that Geoffrey had given him yesterday afternoon. Geoffrey's twelve lines were there, in his looped, childish handwriting, but there was another verse as well now. Lee had written it himself when he got home. It had taken him almost all the evening to get it right.

Mr Merton pulled his reading glasses out of his pocket and slid them onto his nose. Then he started to read the poem out loud, as if he'd never seen it before.

'Feet

When you are young, they bounce along
Where you want to go.
Boot your ball and jump the wall,
Run and kick and grow.

Later on, the road seems long
And your feet are not so new.
They may grow sore, but you've got no more –
They have to take you through.

When you are old, your toes get cold
And arthritis strikes, and gout.
It's easy to lose your dancing shoes
When your feet can't skip about.'

When he got that far, he stopped, as if he was surprised to see that he hadn't reached the end. And Lee carried on with the new last verse, from memory.

'But even if your feet get stiff,
There's plenty left to do.
Life isn't all about kicking a ball,
And grown-ups can have fun too.'

'Hmm,' said Mr Merton. He ran his finger over the paper. Then he said abruptly. 'Know what I did this morning? Before I came to school?'

Lee shook his head.

Mr Merton looked at him, solemnly. 'I got out my trombone and practised all my scales.'

'Your *trombone?*' Lee said. Startled.

Mr Merton nodded. 'I used to be quite a good trombonist, but it's a while since I played.' His mouth twitched. 'I expect that sounds pretty boring to you.'

'We-ell – ' Lee said. He didn't want to

be rude, but it did sound horribly boring.

Mr Merton's mouth twitched again. 'I thought that too. When I was eleven.'

Lee looked at him. 'And what do you think – now?'

'It was very enjoyable,' Mr Merton said. 'Even more fun than football.' Lee looked at him sharply, but his face was perfectly stiff and solemn. He put a hand into his pocket and pulled something out. 'I don't expect you to believe that though. Not while you're eleven. So you'll probably find this more use than a trombone.'

And he held out a new brown shoelace.

Lee hesitated.

'Go on,' Mr Merton said. 'You won't be able to play football properly at playtime. Not if your shoes won't lace up.'

'F-football?' Lee said. 'But we're not allowed – '

'Didn't you see the line across the middle of the playground? Dividing it in half?'

'Yes, but – '

'Well, that's half for the little ones, to keep them safe, and half for you to play football in.'

Lee took a deep breath. 'You mean – not just today? Every playtime?'

'As long as you stay in the right half,' Mr Merton said. His pale face was still stiff. 'Of course, if you go over the line, you'll lose your ball. Just the same as before.'

Then he smiled. Not a little smile. A great grin that spread all the way across his face. The grin that Lee had thought he'd never see again.

'Come on,' he said. 'I'll make an exception and give you back that ball of yours – just this once. Come up to the stockroom and get it.'

'I – ' Lee stared up at him, wondering what to say.

And then he saw that he didn't need to say anything. Somehow, everything had turned out right.

'Thanks,' he said.

'Thank *you*,' Mr Merton said.

And the two of them walked off up the corridor, to fetch the football.

Also by Gillian Cross
SAVE OUR SCHOOL

Bennett School isn't the best school in the world, but Clipper, Spag and Barny are sure it's a lot better than the school they'll have to go to if Bennett is knocked down. So, with their unusual talents they draw up an astonishing plan of action to save the school. But all their stunts seem to go wrong somehow, and it looks as if Bennett School will be knocked down after all . . .

SWIMATHON!

For the first time ever, Barny Gobbo is stuck for a Good Idea – just when money is urgently needed to repair the school minibus. The answer comes when a rival school issues a team swimming challenge. But Barny has reckoned without the bombshell Clipper and Spag are about to drop . . .

THE TREE HOUSE

Sprog was four, and William was seven, and their new house was brand-new. But the tree at the bottom of the garden was a hundred years old.

The two boys long to have a tree house, but their father has to go abroad before he can complete it. However, every month he sends a parcel with something special for the tree house – but will he be back in time to eat the chestnuts like he did when he was a child.

A lyrical, tender family story full of humour and touching detail by the winner of the Carnegie Medal, the Whitbread Award and the Smarties Grand Prix.